**When that broad frame had walked back into her office the other day she'd felt a familiar ache. The one that would be there whether she was pregnant or not.**

This was a guy she'd connected with. This was a guy who could make her burst with happiness one second and have her spitting feathers the next.

He was hot. But he was so much more than hot. She felt safe around him. She felt special. She loved the little twinkle in his bright blue eyes that he seemed to save just for her.

The connection felt real. The connection felt *so* real. And it was the one she'd been waiting for. The one that other people in love had told her would happen one day.

And now it had. In a set of circumstances she couldn't have imagined.

Why couldn't her special guy be someone ordinary…someone normal? Not some hotshot pilot who constantly tried to conquer the world. Not some guy with career ambitions that could leave you breathless.

She banged her head back against the wall. But that was all part of Austin. All part of the guy who had stolen her heart. The guy she'd fallen in love with.

Dear Reader,

This year I had the joy and pleasure of taking my children to the Kennedy Space Center in Florida. I don't know who was more excited—me or them.

I *loved* it. I loved everything about it. We even had the pleasure of meeting a real-life astronaut, Don Thomas, a veteran of four space flights and a man who has spent forty-four days in space. He was gracious, interesting, and he answered all my kids' questions. How could I *not* write about a hero who was an astronaut?

There's something spectacular about this kind of hero. It was great fun having him figure out if his heart lay in the stars or on earth.

My ambition for this book was to get the words 'space baby' in the title. I didn't quite get my way. Maybe next time. I'm sure I have another astronaut hero I can use…

I love to hear from readers. Please feel free to contact me at scarlet-wilson.com.

Love,

*Scarlet Wilson*

# THE DOCTOR'S BABY SECRET

BY
SCARLET WILSON

Published in Great Britain 2016
By Mills & Boon, an imprint of HarperCollins*Publishers*
1 London Bridge Street, London, SE1 9GF

© 2016 Scarlet Wilson

ISBN: 978-0-263-26428-9

Printed and bound in Great Britain
by CPI Antony Rowe, Chippenham, Wiltshire

**Scarlet Wilson** wrote her first story aged eight and has never stopped. She's worked in the health service for twenty years, trained as a nurse and a health visitor. Scarlet now works in public health and lives on the West Coast of Scotland with her fiancé and their two sons. Writing medical romances and contemporary romances is a dream come true for her.

Visit the Author Profile page at millsandboon.co.uk for more titles.

This book is dedicated to my good friend Frances Mason,
my partner in crime, lunch buddy
and one of the bravest women I know.

And to all those brave men and women
who make that journey into the stars.

# CHAPTER ONE

'HERE YOU GO, Dr Carter. Your successful candidates.'

Corrine's heart gave a little flutter at the sight of the four buff folders in front of her. This was one of the best parts of her job. Of the thousands of applications received from a wide range of people—both civilian and military—only a few were chosen for the intensive Astronaut Candidate Programme. She smiled and fingered the folders on her desk. These applicants had gone through weeks of intensive interviews and medical and psychological screening. As part of the medical team at the Worldwide Science and Space Agency, Corrine had already met some of the successful candidates.

'Where am I going, then?'

Every candidate got told in person if they'd been successful by a member of the team at WSSA. She'd been here three years and had been waiting for the chance to do this. The training programme only accepted applications every few years.

Her secretary handed her the schedule. 'California, Washington, Idaho and Nevada.'

Her colleague Blair stuck his head around the door. 'You got yours too?' He was carrying his folders in his arms. 'Who did you get?' He crossed the office in two strides and spread the folders out to see the names.

Almost immediately he started laughing.

'What? What is it?' Corrine looked at the names in front of her. Three were familiar to her. One was a civilian school teacher. One a marine. One an engineer. Blair picked up the last folder before she even had a chance to read the name.

'You got the Top Gun? Good luck with him.'

She snatched the folder back out of his hand. 'The Top Gun?' She stared at the name, Austin Mitchell. There were so many candidates there was no chance of meeting them all. She frowned. 'What's wrong with Austin Mitchell, then?' She opened his folder and started flicking through the pages. Distinction. Merit. Top scores on just about all his testing. The guy seemed more or less perfect.

Blair shook his head and laughed again. 'You'll see.'

Austin checked his instruments one final time and gave a cheeky smile.

'Bates, don't you dare,' came over the intercom.

His laughter had already started. Some traditions would never die. He was already descending for landing—he just wasn't exactly over the landing strip he should be.

'Bates, I'm warning you...'

The adrenaline was coursing through his body—just as it always did when he got behind the controls of a plane. But this wasn't just any plane. This was a brand-new prototype of the F-35. A modified stealth bomber. People wouldn't even hear it coming until it was directly overhead. Including his colleagues in the control tower.

He gave a final check of his instruments—he was the only aviator in the sky right now. The way was clear.

As he positioned the plane he glanced around the surrounding area. There was a reason the Top Gun aviators trained in the middle of the Nevada desert. No one to disturb.

There was a little speck on the landscape ahead. A member of the military personnel headed towards the tower. He hoped they were prepared.

He manoeuvred the F-35 into perfect position. 'He's doing it again, folks. Hold onto your coffee cups.' There was a resigned sigh over the intercom.

'Yee-haw!' he yelled as he passed twenty feet above the tower. Buzzing the tower was one of the perks of the job. Maybe not for them—but definitely for him. And if his luck played out the way he hoped it would, this could be his last time.

She was halfway up the stairs when the noise wave hit. The plane had passed overhead in the blink of an eye. They didn't call them stealth bombers for nothing. Her fingers tightened their grip on the rail just as the whole building rattled and the noise washed over her.

Did people still do that crazy stuff? Surely that was just for the movies?

The sand swirled around her, pulling her carefully styled bun out of its pins and sending stray tendrils across her eyes along with a choking mouthful of sand. She coughed and spluttered, then tried to brush some of the sand off her black knee-length skirt and jacket.

Ignoring the slight shake of her legs, she thumped up the rest of the stairs and keyed in her security code, throwing the door wide. 'Who is that idiot?' she yelled.

All heads in the room turned towards her. She gulped. Not exactly the best entrance in the world.

One of the controllers stood up and walked towards her. 'And you are?'

It was clear she had security clearance or she wouldn't

be here. That didn't mean that anyone would know who she was.

She covered her mouth, coughing again, and stared at his outstretched hand. She reached into her bag and pulled out some sanitiser, giving her hands a quick rub before she shook his hand. 'Hi, I'm Dr Corrine Carter from the Worldwide Science and Space Agency. I'm looking for Austin Mitchell. I believe he's one of the instructors.' She gestured back towards the gate. 'They sent me over here.'

There was the tiniest raise of his eyebrow, but he disguised it well. The guy gave a nod and a firm shake of her hand. 'Luke Kennedy, Air Force Controller.'

The motion caused a sprinkling of sand to land on the carpet. She bit her bottom lip and took off her jacket, giving it another shake. Windswept and dishevelled wasn't exactly the look she wanted when she told the candidate of his success. She held up her hand and shook her head. 'What on earth was that about? Surely these guys are past all the cheap stunts?'

She looked around the office, trying to guess which one of the uniformed personnel was Austin—the guy who'd aced practically every test during the astronaut application procedures.

Her eyes were drawn to a plane landing on the adjacent runway. The plane that had nearly made her land on her butt in the corridor.

Luke Kennedy smiled. He followed her line of sight. 'It's kind of a tradition for the Top Gun instructors.'

'Doesn't it drive you crazy?' She stared at a few tiny blotches of coffee on his shirt.

'Oh, it drives me crazy all right.' His accent was so thick it was almost a drawl. 'You said you were looking for Bates? I mean, Lieutenant Commander Mitchell?'

She nodded, then frowned. 'Bates? Why do you call

him Bates?' She glanced at the file in her hand. 'That isn't in his medical file.'

His smile reached from ear to ear. 'It's his call sign. I'll let you find out for yourself why he's called that.' He pointed across the tarmac to the plane on the far side. 'Well, I guess you found him. Give him a few minutes. He'll take the plane back to the hangar.'

Corrine's mouth fell open. 'That's him?' She gestured towards the plane, which had safely landed and was slowly making its way back to the hangar.

Luke Kennedy turned back to his chair. 'That's him all right. Good luck.'

She bit her lip. That was the second person to wish her luck talking to Austin Mitchell. What was with this guy?

She put her jacket back on and left the control tower. One of the ground crew gave her the go-ahead to cross the tarmac and enter the hangar.

This was her last candidate. The teacher had cartwheeled down the corridor of the school she worked at when she'd got the news she'd been accepted. The engineer had stood up and announced his success to all his colleagues to much celebration. Even her marine had whoop-whooped when he'd been told and then proceeded to jump off one of the pieces of training equipment and body surf across the upheld arms of his colleagues. What would a Top Gun instructor do?

This guy was a little unusual. He hadn't just been selected because he was a pilot—he'd also been selected because he had a master's degree in microbiology. It seemed he'd completed his studies and immediately signed up for the navy doing two tours of duty in Afghanistan as a pilot before being selected for the Top Gun programme.

Lots of the work on the International Space Station was research based. Experiments could be carried out in a non-gravity environment with cells reacting in different ways. This guy wouldn't just be able to pilot, he'd also be able to take a lead on some of the experiments on board. He would be a real asset to the team.

She could see the heat rising from the tarmac as she crossed it. The sand was still whipping past her eyes. What on earth had she done with her sunglasses? The heat in the Nevada desert was stifling. An uncomfortable trickle of sweat ran between her shoulder blades. It didn't matter what the TV adverts said—no antiperspirant could work here.

The walk to the hangar was longer than she expected. Corrine liked to keep up a pristine appearance. Working at one of the most respected agencies in the world meant she constantly felt the need to keep up appearances. But the swirling sand and winds seemed to have other ideas for her.

Her footsteps echoed as she stepped into the hangar. She squinted as her eyes tried to adjust from the glaring sun to the darkened hangar. The place was surprisingly quiet.

A shadow caught her eye. A guy in grey overalls pushing a set of steps away from the plane that had just entered.

She walked swiftly towards it. Her footsteps slowed. The pilot hadn't left the aircraft. He was walking around it, touching it, talking softly under his breath as he did so. She smiled. She'd heard that pilots became attached to their planes but she'd always thought that was an urban myth— something reserved for the bomber pilots of years gone by.

Her eyes finally adjusted to the gloom. He had his helmet in one hand and she could see the embroidery on his flight suit.

She planted a hand on her hip. 'Well, Lieutenant Commander Mitchell, I guess you had better tell me why your call sign is Bates.'

\* \* \*

He'd spotted her as soon as she entered the hangar and listened to the click of her heels as she'd crossed the concrete.

The sight was a little unusual for around here. He usually flew with a female radio intercept officer. But Morah was always dressed in her flight suit—he didn't think he'd ever seen her in a skirt. Certainly not a skirt like this. One that accentuated the flare of her hips and drew attention to a pair of very shapely legs.

His lips curled upwards. The black suit was smart. Appropriate. Covering every single part that should be covered but revealing every curve. The pink silk shirt strained slightly across her breasts, willing him to tug it out from where it was tucked in around her waist. Then it could be equally as dishevelled as her windswept hair.

He'd known why she was here from the second he'd seen her. People didn't visit Naval Air Station Fallon without good reason. It was too hot. Too inaccessible.

He'd met a lot of people at WSSA during his application process. But he'd never met her before—he'd have remembered.

Her skin was gleaming with the compulsory sheen of sweat that everyone around here permanently wore. He gave a little smile as she neared. His hand was still touching the body of the plane. He always did this. Part of his ritual. Didn't matter how mundane or routine some of the flying might be, he always gave a little thanks when he reached the ground safely.

Two tours of duty had made him appreciate life. As a Top Gun instructor he wasn't expected to tour again. He was expected to train other pilots to be the best they could be. He'd trained forty so far. But as much as he loved to fly, as much as he loved the buzz, space had always been his ultimate goal. Now, finally, it was almost in his grasp.

Maybe it was the fact that he knew what she was about to say. Failure had never been an option for him. But something about this woman made him stop and stare. Stop, and almost hold his breath. He could practically see little sparkling stars around this beauty. She looked like a movie-star princess. And since when did he ever think like that?

It must be the moment. The expectation that he was finally on the threshold of his ultimate goal. It couldn't possibly be anything else.

He smiled at the sound of her voice. She had a twang he'd never heard before. Cute.

He spun around to face her just as a soft waft of her perfume drifted across the hot air between them. It wasn't the usual kind of perfume. More citrusy, with an edge of spice.

He kept chewing his gum. It helped him concentrate on training exercises. Even in the dim light of the hangar he could see she was a knockout. The curves had been visible from afar, but up close and personal she was younger than he thought. Fresh, unlined skin with a little touch of make-up. She probably hadn't reckoned on the total sunblock she should be wearing in Nevada. Her blonde hair was straight in some parts, curled in others, with one part that seemed determined to flap around her eyes. It was obviously driving her crazy.

He gave the plane a final tap and stepped towards her. He couldn't help the smile that formed on his face. 'Call signs are kind of personal. You'll have to know me a whole lot better before I tell you why I'm called Bates.'

He probably shouldn't have done it. But he couldn't resist the teasing edge in his voice. Who wouldn't want to flirt with a woman who looked like this?

A hint of colour appeared in her cheeks. But instead of looking uncomfortable she was staring him straight in the eye. It seemed as though the mystery lady liked a challenge—a bit like himself.

She held out her hand towards him. 'Dr Corrine Carter, part of the medical assessment team at WSSA.'

A doctor. Interesting. Maybe she was a little older than she actually looked. WSSA wouldn't take a newbie just out of school. There had to be some experience under that non-existent belt.

Her handshake was firm. She was used to working with military staff and obviously used to holding her own. He pulled his hand back and folded his arms across his chest. She wasn't military, she was civilian. There was no need to salute.

'So, what can I do for you, Dr Carter?' He liked the way that sounded, the way it rolled off the tongue. He could get used to saying that. If she was conscious of his eyes skimming her figure she didn't flicker. Instead she stood for a second, her gaze pointedly holding his before she took a long time looking down the length of his body and then moving up slowly across his chest, shoulders and head again. *Kaboom.*

She was playing him at his own game. He liked her more already.

She kept talking. 'I don't believe we met during your assessment process.' She gave a little wave of her hand. 'Or maybe we did and I've just forgotten.'

He could feel the immediate surge of adrenaline. She was baiting him—deliberately. Letting him think that he was forgettable. He didn't have any doubt that she would have remembered him, just as he would have remembered her.

She straightened her shoulders, unwittingly thrusting her chest towards him. 'But I'm here today and have the greatest pleasure in letting you know that you've made it through the astronaut selection process and have been selected as one of the candidates. Congratulations, Lieutenant Commander Mitchell.'

She didn't look as if this was the greatest pleasure of her life. Instead the end of her nose had started to turn slightly pink—as if the Nevada sun had managed to do its damage already. And the words sounded rehearsed—even a little forced.

'Thanks,' he said briskly as he turned to walk away. His stomach gave a little flip. It didn't matter that this was the news he'd been waiting to hear since he was eight years old. It didn't matter that he'd taken the time to follow in his father's and grandfather's footsteps, becoming a navy pilot first. It didn't matter that his other big love—microbiology—had taken a back seat for the last few years. Astronaut training had always been the golden ticket, the ultimate goal.

In all his dreams of this moment, he had imagined himself with a squadron of men, yelling and whooping at the news. But this day was a little different from what he'd expected. He'd been confident. He'd been sure he would qualify. He knew he'd aced most of the tests and he was at his peak of fitness right now. There wasn't a single medical reason to keep him on this planet.

So, why wasn't he being more gracious about this?

It was that dang woman. She was causing crazy, distracting thoughts in his head. He was thrown off his game. Austin Mitchell was used to being completely in control. Usually everyone around him was singing to his tune. Dr Carter seemed like the kind of woman who was only interested in her own tune. She wouldn't be swayed by a duet with him. And that kind of irked too. Austin Mitchell always got the girl.

'Lieutenant. Lieutenant!' The last one was a yell. He

could hear the rapid fire of her stiletto heels across the concrete. It almost sounded like a run.

Her hand reached for his shoulder and she pulled him around sharply. Being manhandled by a woman. This was a first. And he liked it.

Fire was sparking from her eyes. 'I wasn't finished.'

Wow. He liked her like this. All simmering rage, with colour flushing into her cheeks. He knew he could be infuriating. He'd infuriated everyone from janitors to admirals, and all the people in between. He gave a nonchalant shrug. 'Sorry, I thought you were.'

She sucked in a breath and drew herself up. It was all he could do not to allow his eyes to divert to those straining breasts. Pink satin really suited her skin tone and complemented the dark suit.

She thrust a large brown envelope towards him. 'Your papers with your instructions. You've to report to Houston, Texas at zero eight hundred hours on August the tenth.' She inclined her head a little. 'I trust you are able to follow instructions.'

He gave a little smile. 'Only the important ones.'

She folded her arms across her chest. 'Lieutenant, do you know that as an astronaut trainee you're assigned an overseeing officer?'

He blinked. He'd researched just about everything, but this was something he'd forgotten about in amongst all the other stuff. He gave a brief nod. 'Of course.'

She smiled. A wide, slightly wicked smile that made her eyes gleam. 'You'll be pleased to hear you've got the toughest officer of all.'

'And who might that be?'

She raised her eyebrows. 'Oh, that, Lieutenant Commander, would be me. See you in Houston.' And she turned on her heel and left.

# CHAPTER TWO

AUSTIN PULLED UP a stool next to Michael at the bar and they clinked their beer bottles together. 'Here's to the next eighteen months.' Michael smiled. He hadn't stopped smiling since they'd met a few hours ago—he was still getting over the delight of being selected for the programme.

Austin took a long slow drink of his beer. The bar was packed. And judging from the photos on the walls it seemed it was a long-time favourite of the astronauts based in Houston, Texas. He tried not to stare but it was difficult—he'd followed the careers of most of these astronauts at one point. He'd even done a school project on the first moon landing. Space had always been the dream and these guys were his real-life heroes.

A tune started cranking out from the old-style jukebox in the corner of the room. It was probably older than him and he couldn't help but smile as the lyrics of 'You've Lost that Lovin' Feelin'' echoed around the room. There were murmurs beside him as people started to sing along.

The door swung open, letting in a bright streak of orange sunset. He recognised the silhouette straight away. Curves, curves and more curves.

She was wearing a dark suit similar to the one she'd had on the other day. A one-button jacket accentuating her waist and breasts and a knee-skimming skirt. Her blonde hair was smooth and sleek today—he thought he preferred it windswept and interesting, as it had been that first day.

She walked straight over to the bar and nodded at the barman, who seemed to know her drink. He set down a glass in front of her, which she picked up before heading off to one of the booths to sit next to the other instructors.

Michael bumped his elbow. 'Which one is she, then?'

Austin took another swig of beer. 'That's Dr Corrine Carter—one of the medical team.'

Michael frowned. 'Corrine Carter. That's quite a sharp name. Sounds edgy.'

Austin watched as she glided into the leather seats in the booth. 'I don't think so,' he said smoothly. 'It looks all curves to me.'

The bartender came back and smiled. 'Well, I guess it's you, then.'

The two heads turned to him. 'What do you mean?' asked Michael.

The bartender nodded at Austin. 'Every year, one of the astronaut candidates asks one of the instructors to dance. It's a tradition.' He smiled at Austin. 'Looks like it's going to be you.'

Austin shook his head. 'I don't think so.'

One of the other candidates—Taryn—leaned on the bar. She nodded. 'I think I've heard of this before.' Her eyes connected with Austin's. 'I think he's serious.' She glanced over at Corrine and smiled as she took a swig of her drink. 'What's wrong, Bates, you scared?'

Every other candidate's head turned. It seemed as if the bartender had their full attention.

Austin tried not to smile. The girl was good. She already knew how to press all his buttons. He'd have to watch her in future.

The bartender laughed. He must have seen this all before. And Taryn almost made it sound like a dare. 'Just be thankful for equal opportunities.' He winked at Austin. 'One year it was all male candidates and all male instructors.'

The candidates around burst out laughing as Austin pushed the bar stool back and stood up. He put his bottle of beer back on the bar. He glanced over at Corrine. She was in mid conversation with her colleagues, her blonde hair sitting perfectly on her shoulders. She'd slipped off her jacket and was wearing a pale blue short-sleeved fitted shirt. He could see her defined, tanned arms and her long fingers playing in the condensation on the side of her glass. That simple act sent little pulses to places it shouldn't.

He raised his eyebrows, straightened his uniform and gave a cheeky smile to his colleagues. 'I'm never one to step away from a challenge,' he said confidently.

His colleagues whoop-whooped around him. It was bravado. But only he knew that. He was pretty sure what was going to happen next.

Michael grinned. 'Watch out, Bates. That's a slippery slope you're on.'

Austin blinked and took a final drink of his beer. 'I know,' he said, smiling as he walked over to the booth.

She'd seen him as soon as she'd entered the bar. It was amazing how supersonic your vision could become when you focused on not looking at someone. *Really* focused on not looking at someone. It was much harder than you thought.

The gin wasn't nearly as refreshing as she wanted it to be. Usually just a few sips made her chill. Tonight she was wound up tighter than a coiled spring. She shuffled along next to the other instructors, slipped off her suit jacket and tried to focus on what they were saying.

'His points were off the chart.'

'He really scored that highly?'

She took another sip of her gin. 'Who are we talking about?'

'Bates. Austin Mitchell. Also known as Superboy.'

Great. Perfect. The last person she wanted to talk about. 'I wouldn't exactly call him a boy.'

Marcia, one of the other instructors, raised her eyebrows. 'Really? Then just what would you call him?'

The other instructors started laughing good-humouredly. Frank, the guy on her left, nudged her. 'You gave him the news—how was he?'

Corrine tried not to look flustered and she remembered exactly how he'd looked in that dark hangar with his smouldering eyes. 'A pain in the neck. He's too confident.'

'Aren't they all?' Marcia laughed.

Corrine shook her head. 'No. Not at all. Lisa Kravitz the school teacher—she didn't expect it at all. She was totally stunned. Lewis Donnell, the marine—he and his whole unit couldn't have made more noise if they'd tried.'

Marcia looked at her curiously. 'So what did Bates do that was so different?'

Corrine licked her lips. The mixture of gin and cherry ChapStick wasn't exactly enticing. She was still annoyed by his less than enthusiastic reaction. 'Nothing. That was exactly the point. Nothing. It was like he'd expected it all along. I mean, there's no way anyone could be that confident. There are a thousand different reasons a candidate wouldn't be selected for the programme.'

Adam—the oldest instructor and a former astronaut himself—gave a secret kind of smile. 'I don't know. Sometimes that's the best attitude. The winning attitude. You don't have room in your mind to think it won't actually happen.'

Corrine sighed and ran her finger around the edge of her glass. She'd changed her mind about the gin. A spritzer would have hit the mark much better. She reached over for an empty wine glass on the table and filled it up with some white wine sitting in a cooler next to Marcia.

'What's the deal with the call sign anyway? Shouldn't it be something much cooler?'

'Like what?' Frank took a swig of his beer and shifted in his seat.

'You know, like Maverick or Viper or Cougar or... Lightning.' She was grasping at straws now.

Frank shook his head. 'You watch way too many movies, Corrine.'

She shrugged her shoulders. 'But why Bates? It's not anything like his name. And it's kind of boring.'

Frank laughed. 'Oh, that's easy.' Then he shook his head. 'And it's certainly not boring.'

She wrinkled her nose. Frank had been a Top Gun instructor too. Maybe it was some weird navy thing she didn't know about.

He held out his hand towards her. 'Let me expand it a little for you. Bates. *Norman Bates.*'

Corrine blinked and glanced from person to person around the table. Everyone else seemed to have caught on immediately. 'What do you mean? That he's crazy?'

The others started to laugh.

'But that's impossible. Our pilots undergo complete psychological evaluations. We can't have anyone that's a risk taker. That could compromise the mission.'

Adam shook his head. 'Oh, he's not crazy. But he's made some of the gutsiest flight moves I've ever seen. That's how he earned his call sign. And we need people that can make good decisions under pressure—even when it seems like the chips are down. If Austin Mitchell makes it to the space station I think he'll be a great asset to our programme.' He raised his glass. 'I'd even take bets on him making it.'

Marcia shook her head. 'I'm not taking that bet. He's too good.'

Frank shook his head too. 'Me either. I know a shoo-in when I see one.'

Corrine started to get annoyed. Everyone seemed to think this guy was great. They hadn't seen the gleam of arrogance in his eyes. The one that had prickled her senses in all the wrong places. There were some catcalls from the other side of the bar. A little tremor danced down her spine but there was no way she was turning around.

'Uh-oh.' Marcia smiled as she pushed her glass around the table. 'It looks like Superboy is on his way over.'

She couldn't help it. Corrine turned towards the bar. Austin Mitchell was walking straight towards them. No. Straight towards *her*. His eyes locked with hers. That darn white uniform showed off the width of his shoulders and chest. The gold on his epaulettes gleamed at her. But the thing that freaked her out most was the confident grin on his face.

He held out his hand towards her as he gave a brief nod to the others at the table. 'Dr Carter. Would you like to dance?'

Her mouth almost fell open. It was right up there with things least likely to expect.

She almost choked. 'What?' She could hear a stifled snigger behind her.

She looked around the bar. The music was audible, but low—and there was no dance floor. It just wasn't that kind of place.

His bright blue eyes were fixed on hers. She hadn't been able to see them properly in the dark hangar. Which was probably just as well, because right now she was getting the full hypnotic effect. The artificial lights in the bar seemed perfect for showing them at their best.

'Dance,' he said calmly, as if she'd misunderstood.

There was a nudge at her back. Frank was almost willing her to go. But the nudge lit a little flare inside her. How dared he? How dared he approach her so directly in front of all her colleagues—his instructors—and practically ask her out? Didn't the guy have any decorum?

'No,' she said quickly. 'I don't want to dance.' She couldn't hide the disdain in her voice. The coil inside was tightening. She'd wanted to relax tonight—not put herself in an uncomfortable position.

Her earlier comment about him not being a boy had already been misinterpreted by her colleagues. Now, they might actually think something was going on. That was the last thing she needed. She'd only been at WSSA for a few years. This was her first astronaut candidate selection. Her position and job meant everything to her. She'd put her life on hold for it. She didn't want anything to interfere.

Austin was still standing smiling at her. It was almost as if he hadn't heard her say no.

She stood up quickly and tugged at her skirt, pulling it back into position. She gave him a sharp stare. 'That would be a no, Lieutenant Commander Mitchell. Now, if you'd excuse me, myself and your other instructors need to have conversations that you can't be party to.'

She gave him a nod as she brushed past. It was important that he respect her position on the team. It was important that he realised she wouldn't be compromised. No matter how good he looked in that uniform. She could see all the expectant faces of the rest of the candidates in the background. They were watching with interest. Waiting to see what she would do. Did any of them actually think she might say yes?

The hairs on his arms came into contact with her skin. *Ignore it.* Her brain repeated the message as she walked towards the ladies' room. Her skin was on fire. A thousand little caterpillars were currently marching across that tiny patch of skin. She couldn't help it—her other hand automatically reached across and rubbed it as she banged the ladies' room door open with her hip.

Cold water. That was what she needed right now. Anything that would stop the persistent fire caused by Austin Mitchell from circulating around her body.

There was a whoop behind him as Corrine brushed past him as if he didn't exist. He'd seen it. That little flicker in her eyes. It wasn't panic. She wasn't the type. The disbelief he'd almost expected, but hesitation he hadn't. Was there the tiniest chance she might have said yes?

He shrugged and gave a rueful smile to the other instructors. Adam winked. He knew exactly what was going on. Traditions didn't just exist amongst Top Gun pilots—WSSA candidates had a whole book of their own.

Frank stood up. 'Excuse me, folks. Back in a bit.' His face looked a bit pinched.

Austin watched him head to the gents'. Was he annoyed with him? He moved back and put a twenty on the bar. 'Get another round,' he said to Michael.

Michael lifted the twenty and waved to the bartender. 'Crashed and burned.' He laughed at Austin. 'Get used to it. Corrine Carter looked mad.'

Austin stared at the swinging door of the gents'. It was weird. His parents used to tease him as a kid—they'd told him that his spider sense was tingling whenever he'd had an instinct about things. They'd learned quickly he was always right—even when everything seemed fine. It had served him well on his tours of duty and on his test flights. Knowing when something just wasn't quite right with a plane or mission had saved him on more than one occasion.

And tonight his spider sense was busy creating a full-on web.

He strode towards the gents'. What was the worst that could happen? Frank would tear a few strips off him for his stunt. He was a big boy. He could take it easily.

The door swung open. Frank hadn't even made it to a cubicle. His hand was leaning on the wall above one of the urinals. Austin quickly averted his eyes—last thing he needed to do was watch another man take a leak.

But his instincts were on overtime. Darn it. He looked again. Frank hadn't even managed to unzip his trousers. His other hand was resting on his chest.

'Frank? You okay?'

He made it just in time. The guy's legs crumpled beneath him and Austin caught him as he made a slow descent to the floor. Frank was no lightweight—he must have been around twenty stone—but Austin could handle it.

He eased him onto the floor and laid him on his back. Hell. What next?

He didn't have any advanced medical training, just the basic navy first-aid course.

Part of the WSSA training would be about emergency medical situations like this—it seemed he was starting early.

Frank's colour was terrible, a mixture of translucent and grey, with a slight blue tinge around his lips. Austin bent his head to Frank's chest, listening and watching for any rise and fall. He pressed his fingers to Frank's carotid pulse. Nothing. He moved them. Maybe he wasn't in the right place?

'I need some help in here,' he yelled.

He tipped Frank's head back and steeled himself. Mouth-to-mouth with a guy. Just as well he didn't have time to think about this. He pinched his nose and covered Frank's mouth with his, breathing out once and then twice.

The door banged open to his side. He didn't even look up.

'What the…?' Corrine's voice tailed off immediately.

He could almost see the instant recognition in her eyes and the work-mode focus coming into play. 'Ambulance, now,' she shouted over her shoulder before crossing the floor in a few long strides.

She didn't miss a beat, just hitched up her skirt—giving him a generous shot of thigh—and knelt down beside him. It took her only a few seconds to do her own assessment. Her eyes met his. 'Right, Lieutenant Commander Mitchell, let's see how good you are.'

Her heart was thudding against her chest. When she'd heard the call for help she'd moved immediately—even though she hadn't recognised the voice.

It had a taken a couple of seconds to comprehend the sight of Austin leaning over Frank and kissing him before her medical senses had taken hold.

Frank looked awful. Why hadn't she noticed anything earlier? Why hadn't he told her he felt unwell?

Everything was automatic from that point onwards. Airway clear, breathing absent, circulation absent. She pushed aside everything personal. She loved Frank. He was one of the kindest, nicest guys she'd ever worked with. It would be so easy to be emotional. But she couldn't let herself be. She always had to put a wall between herself and the patient she was treating—it couldn't be personal. Not in any way at all.

As for Lieutenant Commander Mitchell? She needed a partner in crime right now. And it seemed it would have to be him. None of the other medical staff were here. She was Frank's best chance and that was all she could focus on.

She positioned herself above the chest, kneeling on the hard floor and crossing her hands one over the other on Frank's chest. She couldn't even count how many times she'd done this before.

What she really needed was an oxygen supply, IV access, a defibrillator, cardiac monitoring and a whole host of emergency drugs. What she had was herself and Austin Mitchell. And just how much use could a guy be whose call sign was Bates?

'We're going to do thirty to two.'

He blinked and she recognised his confusion.

She started compressions, counting out loud while recognition dawned on Austin's face. This was as up close and personal as they'd got. His face was only a few inches from hers, positioned opposite and above Frank's face. There were a few tiny lines around the corners of his eyes. A shadow along his jaw line and dark lashes around his blue eyes.

On an ordinary day the features of Austin Mitchell would be a lot to admire. Today, she couldn't allow them to distract her.

She got to thirty and stopped for a second. The door swung open as Austin bent automatically to do the two breaths. She had no idea if he had any first-aid experience. But he tilted the head back to the right angle, pinched Frank's nose and covered Frank's mouth with his and breathed out at a steady rate.

'Oh, Frank. No.' Marcia's voice was both shocked and scared. Corrine started compressions again, counting in her head. 'Ask if they've got an AED,' she said automatically. 'A defib,' she added.

'Right.' Marcia disappeared out of the door only to be replaced by Adam and Blair.

She started counting out loud to prepare Austin for his next stint. 'Twenty-seven, twenty-eight, twenty-nine, thirty.' She sat back for a second and took a deep breath.

'Someone find out how long the ambulance will be,' she directed as Austin finished the breaths and sat back. She started counting out loud again. It didn't matter that in theory she knew the person doing the compressions should change every two minutes. There was no way she'd let someone who'd never done this before take over from her. Getting the compressions right was important.

'No defib.' Marcia's pale face appeared in the doorway again. Blair put his arm around her shoulder automatically. Adam gave a little shake of his head. 'I'll wait outside for the ambulance.'

'Six minutes,' came the shout from outside.

Six minutes. She could do that. She was being methodical. Pushing everything else from her brain. This was Frank. The guy with years of experience at WSSA and the most self-deprecating humour. He could find something to joke about even on the darkest of days. But most of all he listened. He'd welcomed her as a new instructor. Shown her all the ropes. Explained the systems, procedures and protocols that could be mind-boggling and sent her in the right direction when things had seemed like a puzzled map of tunnels.

He lived and breathed WSSA. Had done for years. His wife had died of cancer a few years ago and, although he spent his holidays with his grown-up daughter, he was first at work in the morning and last away at night.

There was no way she was going to have to make that *I'm so sorry* call to his daughter, Lucy.

She was praying for a coronary—even a massive one with a clot could be dealt with by an angioplasty and stented if necessary. A pulmonary embolism would—at this stage—have probably caused fatal damage. A stroke could be similar.

The muscles in her arms started to burn a little. It was nothing. She could handle it. A warm hand reached over hers as she counted out loud. 'Want to swap?'

It was probably only a millisecond. But it seemed like so much more. It was the first time she'd recognised sincerity in Austin Mitchell's gaze. On every other occasion his confidence had almost seemed to mock her. But this time it was different. This time she saw a glimmer of the man he actually was instead of the person he showed the world.

His gaze seemed to drift downwards, then he gave his head a little shake and met her eyes again.

She glanced down. It was clear from his position that he had a prime-time view straight down the front of her shirt to her cleavage. At least he'd had the decency to avert his eyes. Austin Mitchell wasn't all face and bravado.

'I'm fine,' she said quickly. 'Just keep going.'

And he did. They worked in unison for the next few minutes. She could hear the voices outside. The other candidates had realised that something was wrong but Blair stood across the doorway and none would dare argue with him. They didn't need to see Frank like this.

Every compression hurt her arms and made her shoulders ache. But she didn't care. She was trying not to let the statistics she knew about MI circulate around her brain. Defibrillation was the best bet. Every minute it was delayed reduced Frank's chances.

There was a shout outside and Adam ran in with the

paramedics behind him. He must have filled them in on who she was because they didn't bombard her with a series of questions. One immediately pulled out the pads for the defibrillator and the other opened the carton of drugs. She ripped open Frank's shirt and let the paramedic place the pads, watching the monitor and praying for a shockable rhythm.

Someone was listening. VF. Ventricular fibrillation. The automated response from the machine filled the air. 'Stand clear, shocking.'

She reached for the IV kit, her eyes not leaving the monitor. Frank's body jerked in response to the shock. The thin green line reappeared, squiggly with no discernible pattern.

'Stand clear, shocking,' the machine said again. The room was silent. Frank's body jerked once again and this time the line was different. It took a few seconds to appear, but this time it was a slow sinus rhythm.

Corrine didn't stop to think. She turned Frank's arm over and quickly inserted a cannula for venous access. They'd need it if he arrested again.

Everything moved like clockwork. Austin sat back, allowing the other paramedic to check the airway and slip an oxygen mask in place as they positioned Frank onto the stretcher.

There was no end of volunteers to help take the stretcher out to the waiting ambulance and Corrine gave one of the paramedics a nod. 'I'll be coming with you.'

He acknowledged her as they lifted Frank into the back of the ambulance. Marcia came over and grabbed her arm. 'Call me as soon as you get there. Adam's already contacting Frank's daughter. We'll let you know when we get her.'

Something prickled at the back of her spine. She looked

at the crowded, anxious faces staring into the back of the ambulance. One was missing.

'Give me a sec,' she shouted to the paramedic as he hooked Frank up to their equipment.

She pushed her way through the crowd. Austin wasn't anywhere in sight.

It only took a few steps to reach the gents' again. He was standing quietly, staring at the floor where Frank had lain and rubbing his hands together. She recognised that look.

She'd seen it numerous times throughout her career. Whether it was a student doctor, a new nurse or even an old-timer exposed to a situation they weren't used to.

She just hadn't expected it from Mr Confidence.

She walked over quickly and stood right under his nose, reaching over and touching his arm. 'Austin?'

He blinked and stepped back. He hadn't even realised she'd entered.

She squeezed his arm. 'You did good. Thanks for your help.' It was all she had time for. She had to leave right now. But her knowledge and experience meant she'd never leave a team member without acknowledging their part.

His blue eyes met hers. Zing. It was like a little thunderbolt. 'Any time,' he murmured quietly as his gaze drifted down to the floor.

Her stomach flip-flopped. Frank was her priority. Frank was all that mattered right now. She nodded and ran back to the door.

Everything else would have to wait.

# CHAPTER THREE

AUSTIN GLANCED AROUND the room. He'd met all the other candidates as they'd arrived over the last two days, but this morning was their first official training day. The room was awash with the signature bright blue flight suits. He'd felt a real surge of pride this morning as he'd put it on.

He'd worked hard for this. Focused hard to finally get to wear the uniform he'd always wanted. He'd snapped a quick pic to send to his mum and dad. That had been around fifteen minutes ago—by now, his mother would have printed out twenty copies to give to all her friends.

All the instructors were standing in front of them. Everyone in the room knew Frank was missing. He'd found a handwritten note from Corrine in his mailbox this morning saying Frank was doing as well as could be expected. His hand slipped into his pocket and he touched the piece of paper. She'd used a purple pen. It had made him smile. Kind of quirky.

Corrine looked tired this morning. She had dark circles under her eyes and he wondered if she'd stayed at the hospital all night with Frank. She was wearing her obligatory dark suit and a pale pink shirt. And because he was sitting in the front row the scent of her perfume was drifting towards him. It was light, but not quite floral, something more vanilla. The kind of scent that made you think something was good enough to eat.

Adam Bailey cleared his throat. 'Guys, I've been where you are. I know how proud you all feel right now and I want you to know that we recognise your achievement of being selected. There were over six thousand applications for the Astronaut Candidate Programme this time around. It's not an easy process to go through—we all appreciate that. But the time for celebration is over.'

He pressed his finger down on the desk in front of him. 'Now is the time for hard work.' He looked around the room. 'Your Astronaut Candidate Training will include scientific and technical briefings, intensive instruction in International Space Station systems, Extravehicular Activity—EVA—robotics, physiological training, T-38 flight training, water and wilderness survival training and medical training. If you can't already do it—you'll have to learn to speak Russian. And your training will be in a variety of settings. You'll be in Kazakhstan and in Russia. You'll be in the Aquarius research station in Key Largo. You'll be in the desert. You'll be in the jungle. And you'll log more hours in the neutral buoyancy lab than you'll want to.'

He turned towards Corrine and the rest of her team. 'You'll already know which doctor has been allocated to you to work with you through your training. These people will get to know you better than you currently know yourself. Use them. Work with them.' He turned back to the candidates. 'While I'd love it if you all ended up in space, the simple fact is that some of you won't. Medical issues can crop up. Life can get in the way. Your focus and commitment is essential to your success in this programme. I expect you all to do your utmost to fulfil your dreams.'

The person next to Austin started clapping. There were a few seconds of awkward silence before others joined in.

The surge of pride went through him as he looked around. God willing, in a couple of years' time he could be spending a few months in space with these people.

The ultimate goal.

He looked along the line of instructors. Three of them had been astronauts. Some were doctors. And others were experts in the types of technology they'd use aboard the space station. Every one of them had something to teach him.

So why did his eyes keep going back to the tired blonde on the platform?

# CHAPTER FOUR

CORRINE SMILED AS she stood at the side of the training pool. She liked early mornings. It was her favourite time. Sipping her coffee as she watched the sunrise was always her favourite part of the day.

There was something so calming about watching the smudges of orange and yellow emerge from the distance. She lived only a few miles from the base in an old clapboard-style house with its own front porch. She'd even managed to find an old rocker for her porch and drank her coffee there every morning. It grounded her. The last eight years had been hard—all driving towards her goal of working at WSSA. Once qualified she'd worked as an emergency medicine specialist for a few years before studying Aerospace Medicine at Dayton, Ohio for two years. There had been no time for fun, no time for relationships and no time for socialising.

At least that was what she told anyone who asked. It seemed simpler.

She didn't want pity. Her first experience had been with a guy much older who had treated her badly. She'd learned quickly—the hard way. She'd escaped with a promptly placed bottle to the back of his skull and vowed never to let herself seem vulnerable again. A few years of self-defence classes had taught her everything she needed to know. Everything had to be on her terms. And every relationship after that had been. Trouble was, most guys didn't like that. And she'd never let herself get truly emotionally involved with any of them.

Now, she had the job of her dreams and the mortgage on a house to match. Who needed a guy? All she needed was a dog.

She folded her arms across her chest as she watched the candidates being briefed at the side of the pool. All candidates were required to complete military water survival before beginning their flying syllabus. They also had to become SCUBA qualified to prepare them for spacewalk training. It was surprising how many of the trainees didn't realise a large percentage of astronaut training was carried out in water. Apart from the fact that they could land in water after their descent back to earth, working in water, timing their missions to coincide with oxygen supplies and learning about buoyancy were all crucial parts of the training.

This morning's session was relatively simple. One of the other instructors was briefing them. She was only there to look after anyone that got into difficulties.

'You'll be required to swim three lengths of the twenty-five-metre pool without stopping, then swim three lengths dressed in your flight suit and tennis shoes. There's no time limit but once you've completed that you're required to tread water continuously for ten minutes wearing your flight suit.'

She saw the anxious glances. This test was pretty well known amongst the candidates—she'd be surprised if any of them hadn't made special arrangements to practise in advance.

The instructor blew his whistle. Almost instantly all the candidates disappeared into the water. Some dives were better than others. Nearly all started in a fast crawl. It didn't really surprise her that Austin Mitchell was right out there in front. Two others favoured the breaststroke. Austin's fellow candidate, Michael, matched him stroke for stroke.

She smiled at the competitive edge. It was good. It kept them motivated and on point. They turned in unison and headed back down the pool.

She tried not to stare. A quick glance around told her no one was watching. It was too easy to see the defined muscles in his back and shoulders. The guy had to spend all his spare time in the gym. Which was good. He would need a defined programme for going to space. And it would be her that would design it for him. It was important that all astronaut candidates were at their peak of physical fitness before they left earth.

Space played havoc with the human body. Astronauts suffered from decreased immunity in space, vision changes, where the fine structures of the eye could be affected by the fluid changes in space, a decrease in bone density and a higher ratio of muscle wastage.

She was a doctor. She was employed to assess their physical fitness. So, why had standing at the side of the pool and watching Austin Mitchell walk from the changing rooms made her feel like some kind of voyeur?

He had the kind of sculpted stomach muscles that most men spent their life dreaming of. Did the guy even eat carbs? She'd need to check his diet with him.

Thank goodness he hadn't been wearing Speedos. The shorts were bad enough.

There was a shout next to her as Austin and Michael emerged from the pool together. The water made his shorts cling to the tight muscles on his thighs and his backside.

As he scrambled into his flight suit he glanced over his shoulder directly towards her.

Caught. Well and truly caught. The tiniest flicker of a smile hinted at his lips as he shoved his wet feet into the tennis shoes. The grin had reached from ear to ear before he dived straight back in.

She blew out a breath as the heat rushed into her cheeks. Darn it!

Her eyes swept the pool, checking on all the other candidates. Everyone seemed fine. Speed wasn't really the issue—even though no one had told those two guys. Completion was the issue. Another instructor was logging times on a tablet near the edge of the pool.

The heat wasn't abating. She fixed her eyes on another few candidates pulling themselves out of the pool and into their flight suits. She was the doctor. She was supposed to be looking at their bodies. She was supposed to be monitoring them for any difficulties. So why did she feel like a teenage girl caught spying on her hunky next-door neighbour?

She walked over to Bill, who was marking times on the tablet. 'Quickest time ever—so far,' he muttered under his breath.

She should be happy that the candidates were performing so well. But because it was Austin Mitchell with his cheeky grin and pert bum it just annoyed her. He and Michael were currently powering up the length of the pool as if they were dressed in just their swimmers. The flight suits and tennis shoes didn't seem to be causing them any problems at all.

'Let's see how good they really are,' she said quietly. She stepped a little closer to the edge of the pool just as Austin completed his third length one second ahead of Michael and punched the air.

They turned and swam away from the edge, ready to start their ten minutes of treading water. It had been a long time since Corrine had done anything like this. She'd had to tread water in pyjamas for a certificate in high school. Even now she could remember how heavy her legs had felt by the end.

Austin swam straight in front of her, his bright blue eyes reflected back from his blue suit and the surrounding water. With his tan and straight white teeth the guy should be in toothpaste commercials.

Why was it that everything about him drove her crazy?

He was just too much of a know-it-all by half. She glanced at Bill and shot him a conspiratorial smile. 'You know, Bill, I've been thinking. Treading water is fine, but men aren't always renowned for their multitasking skills— a vital component for an astronaut. I think we should add some brain strain into this assessment.'

Bill laughed. 'Someone annoyed you today, Dr Carter? Or did they only give you one shot in your coffee this morning?'

Michael and Austin were both treading water in front of her. The guys looked as if they were taking a walk in the park. The flight suits and shoes weren't hampering them at all.

She gave Bill a nod. 'Let's see if these guys can work their muscles and their brains.'

She turned to face the pool again. 'I know you started reading your mountain's worth of training manuals. Let's see how much you've taken in.'

Michael shot Austin a look of panic. They'd only been here a few days and the training manuals would take around a year to master.

Austin's eyes hadn't moved from hers. This guy rarely seemed rattled.

'Tell me about the primary robotics system used on the ISS.'

It was a shot in the dark. The majority of her work was purely clinical with a dash of research thrown in. She knew the basics of the other systems but not the details. That was their job, not hers. But it didn't mean she couldn't keep them on their toes.

'We use the mobile servicing system. The Canadarm2. There's a new one currently in development.' That rich drawl sent an involuntary tremor down her spine—one she pointedly ignored. Austin was still treading away. There was a glimmer of something in his eyes. He knew he was annoying her. It was almost as if it was deliberate. Like a tiny bug getting under her skin.

'Tell me about the maintenance required on ISS.'

'We'll need much longer than ten minutes,' quipped Austin. 'Have you got all night?'

She pressed her lips together. There was no way she was going to blush again. No way at all.

Michael was concentrating too hard to notice the flirtation right in front of him. 'Inside or out?' he asked. 'And what system do you want to start with?'

She nodded towards him, pretending not to hear Bill laughing under his breath. 'Life support systems,' she said quickly.

Austin cut in. 'The environmental control and life support system takes care of atmospheric pressure, fire detection and suppression, oxygen levels, waste management and water supply.'

'And if your oxygen supply fails?'

'There's back-up in the solid fuel oxygen generation canisters. One canister can last a day.'

A few other candidates swam up next to them and started treading water. Austin glanced around and then back to Corrine; his cheeky grin seemed a permanent feature on his face this morning. 'What? You're not going to ask the rest questions too?'

It was a direct barb. He knew she'd been quizzing him because he'd annoyed her. Now she would look unprofessional if she didn't subject the rest of the candidates to the same questions.

Bill threw her a sympathetic glance. 'Let's talk about the different modules.'

She breathed a sigh of relief. There were numerous modules, some pressurised, some not. This could take up valuable time.

She gave him a grateful smile and walked over, watching as he input some data on the tablet. Nearly all the candidates had completed their swim.

Everyone looked good. Some looked better than others. This was typical in a class. Her job was to try and ensure that everyone would be in their peak medical condition by the end of their training. She only had four candidates to design fitness programmes for. That would be her next task. How would Austin Mitchell take to being told what he could and couldn't do?

She bit her lip as her stomach gave a low grumble. Maybe she was being a little cranky. Coffee was distinctly on her mind, anything to cut out the smell from the swimming pool, which would linger in her hair for the rest of the day. She was having strange cravings for a calorie-laden banana loaf. If she was lucky—there would be none in the canteen today. As soon as she got a whiff of one, she'd be sunk, in more ways than one.

'Time!' Bill's voice cut through her thoughts and Austin and Michael high-fived each other in the water then swam to the side.

He could have got out of the pool anywhere. But no.

Austin Mitchell, complete with flight suit and dorky tennis shoes, swam directly underneath her and pulled himself out right under her nose. Water streamed from him, running off the bright blue flight suit and pooling next to her shoes.

She should have chosen her footwear more carefully. This was one of her favourite pairs.

'How'd I do?' That drawl again. Right up close and personal. What was it about that voice? She'd worked with lots of guys from all over the States and a whole host of international guests. Some women loved Italian accents, some Irish. A few women around here had definite preferences for the Russian accent. One of her colleagues was in a long-distance relationship with a cosmonaut. She'd lived in California as a child where accents weren't as noticeable. But Austin's Texas drawl seemed to send a zing around her whole body, connecting with each tiny nerve and catapulting it into overtime.

She licked her lips and kept her voice steady. 'I think you were pretty average.'

He raised one eyebrow. That darn smirk. It was almost as if he saved it for her especially because he knew it would make her crazy. 'Average? I'm average?'

Oh, good. She'd hit a nerve. She liked that. Mr Top Gun was probably too used to being the best at everything. She'd hate it if he lost his competitive edge.

She waved her hand as she tried to keep the teasing tone from her voice. But it was *so* hard. 'We all have different talents, Lieutenant Commander Mitchell. Maybe we've yet to discover yours.'

She walked away, still keeping her eyes on the rest of the candidates in the pool. She couldn't leave until they were all officially finished. Now she was happy she'd worn her favourite heels. She could almost feel his eyes fixated on her swinging hips as she crossed over towards one of the other instructors.

Having a bad experience in the past hadn't made her immune to flirtations or charms. She enjoyed them. She enjoyed meeting men who were happy to see her as an equal partner instead of a conquest. The twinkle in Austin's eyes gave her more than a little buzz.

Blair looked up from his monitor. 'You two are going to drive each other crazy,' he said quietly. 'This is going to be fun to watch.'

She straightened her back. 'I don't know what you mean.'

Blair stared at her. 'Ever thought about applying for the programme yourself? Fancy some time up in space?' He shook his head as he turned the monitor towards her. 'You and him in a confined space for three to six months.' He laughed and blew into his fingertips. 'Boom!'

She leaned forward to look at the results that had been shared from Bill's tablet. 'There's absolutely nothing in it. He's just a new guy trying his luck. They're all overconfident to start with. He'll settle down.' Too bad she didn't believe a single word she'd just said. 'As for space—no way. I'm keeping my feet fixed firmly to the ground. They don't sell Girl Scout cookies in space.'

Blair shook his head again. 'If you say so, Corrine. I'm not the expert in chemistry. I'm just the payload specialist. But when you two are in the same room...' His voice tailed off.

'What?' She couldn't help the edge in her voice. It was bad enough trying to ignore the buzz in her body whenever he was around. The last thing she wanted was for anyone else to notice it too.

Blair gave her a huge grin. 'Let's just say it's best not to have combustible materials in space.' He pointed to the stats. 'And it looks like this guy isn't going to be flunking out.'

She sighed and folded her arms across her chest. Austin had aced it. Not only that—his was the fastest time of any candidate ever. Great. Once he knew that, he'd be even more unbearable. Blair gave a little shrug. 'My guess is he's in it for the long haul.'

She looked over at the pool. The rest of the candidates were just emerging from the water—their ten minutes of treading water over. Her stomach flip-flopped. They were right at the start of the process. How many of them would actually make it into space?

'They're all in it for the long haul,' she said quietly. She reached over and pressed a hand on Blair's shoulder. 'I'll see you later. The benefits of being a doctor mean I've got special permission to see Frank.'

'Tell him I'll visit tomorrow.'

She nodded. 'I will.' She had one last glance across the pool. All the candidates were now stripping out of their flight suits. She hated the fact that her eyes were drawn to one body.

She could tell even from here he was still mad. His jaw was set and he was barely making eye contact with the rest of his colleagues. For all his bravado it seemed that Austin Mitchell ran a little deeper than she'd first suspected. It didn't matter that he and Michael had finished first out of his group of candidates. He'd no idea how previous candidates might have performed and it was obviously playing on his mind.

She couldn't prevent a small smile from playing around her mouth. Finally, she knew which buttons to press with Austin Mitchell.

Useful information. Very useful.

* * *

Frank looked a hundred times better than he had the last time she'd seen him.

His room was filled with yellow flowers and the sun was streaming through the blinds. She nodded at the flowers. 'I thought they were banned from hospitals now.'

He winked at her. 'I have a private room. And a wonderful physician who says there're no problems with my chest.' He shifted on the bed. 'Even though it feels as though someone's been using me as a punchbag.'

She winced as she sat down next to his bed. 'Sorry, Frank. Needs must.'

He rolled his eyes. 'I would much rather you'd been the one doing the mouth-to-mouth instead of Bates.'

She laughed. 'I think he would probably have preferred that too. But have you seen the build of that guy? If I'd let him do CPR he probably would have broken all your ribs.'

Frank leaned over and squeezed her hand. 'Thank you, honey. I won't ever be able to repay you.'

She shook her head as her heart swelled. 'You already have—you're still here. You don't know how grateful I am for that.'

He leaned back against his pillows. 'Guess I'll need to thank Lieutenant Commander Mitchell too.'

She shook her head. 'Don't. It'll only go to his head.'

Frank looked at her carefully. 'Still smarting that he asked you to dance?'

'Of course not.'

But Frank wasn't convinced. He waggled his finger at her. 'I like that. It takes guts.' He paused for a second. 'Anyway, last woman I asked to dance married me.' He gave a little smile. 'She refused the first time too.'

Corrine sat back a little. She'd heard a lot about Frank's

wife and daughter but she'd never heard this. 'Mary refused to dance with you?'

He nodded and held out his hands. 'Apparently I was
too flashy for her. Too confident. She couldn't see that
my knees were knocking under my trousers or that I was
about to be sick on the floor.'

Corrine couldn't stop grinning. When she'd first met
Frank he'd been newly widowed. He'd talked about Mary
all the time and showed her lots of pictures. They'd always
seemed like a match made in heaven. It was kind of fascinating to know that she'd originally turned him down.

'If she said no, how did you manage to persuade her?'

Frank smiled and his gaze drifted off. 'Persistence.
And lots of it.' He took a few seconds then looked back at
her again. 'Austin Mitchell reminds me of myself. I was
exactly the same. Focused. Confident. Smart. Thought I
could rule the world. It took a good woman to show me
different.'

Corrine shifted uncomfortably in her chair. He was giving her that look again. The one that said he had things all
mapped out for her.

She tried to keep things light. 'The candidates in this
rotation are excellent. I just hope they all make it to the
end of the training.' She reached into her bag and pulled
out a plastic container. 'Here. I brought you something.'

Frank put his hand on his chest. 'Oh, no. Tell me you
didn't bake.'

She laughed. Her colleagues had learned quickly that
baking wasn't her best skill—even though she liked to
try. She peeled the lid off the box. 'Of course I did. Low
fat apple, sultana and cinnamon muffins. I thought they
might cheer you up.'

Frank leaned over and looked in the box. They were her

third attempt. The first two had ended up in the trash can. They were uneven and looked a tad lumpy.

He smiled and clicked the lid back on the container. 'Well, it's the thought that counts. Thanks, honey. Now get back to the base. You've got some astronauts to lick into shape.'

The expression changed on his face at his choice of words, then he tipped back his head and laughed as Corrine got to her feet and headed towards the door.

'Watch out, Dr Carter,' he called after her as she scurried down the corridor. 'One of these guys might be lighting up your world in more ways than one!'

Corrine shook her head. Austin Mitchell was already giving her sleepless nights. She just didn't want anyone to know that.

And she certainly didn't need Frank teasing her. Next time she'd make him eat one of her muffins. Or maybe all of them.

# CHAPTER FIVE

She was staring at the trace on the EKG machine. As well as being special monitor for four of the astronaut candidates she also took her turn in the WSSA health centre. She could see any of the personnel from the site that had a medical query.

She frowned at the monitor and walked over to Bruce, one of the tech guys who had just finished in the gym and had come in because he was a little short of breath.

'I'm going to draw some blood.'

'What? Why?' He sat up and swung his legs off the examination bed.

She pressed her arm against his shoulder. 'I didn't say you could get up, did I?'

He frowned and lay back. 'What do you need blood for?'

She gave him a smile. 'I think you're a little unusual.'

The edges of his lips turned upwards. He obviously liked the sound of that.

'What were you doing exactly?'

He shrugged. 'I was training with someone. You know, on the treadmill, on the rowing machine, lifting some weights.'

She nodded. 'When was the last time you ate or drank?'

He frowned and looked at the clock. 'It was a while ago. Breakfast time, around six, I think.'

She gave a little shake of her head. That was six hours ago. 'Did you push yourself more than you normally do?'

Sweat was still running down from his forehead and his shorts and gym vest were already saturated. She'd had to wipe him down to attach the electrodes for the EKG.

He gave a half-smile. 'Sort of. I've been training with one of the new guys. We push each other. He's super fit.'

She frowned. 'Who is it?'

'One of the astronaut candidates. Austin Mitchell.'

There it was. The little surge inside her whenever she heard the name. The guy just seemed to be everywhere. She bit her lip. 'I guess I'll need to have a word with Lieutenant Commander Mitchell.'

She wrapped a tourniquet around Bruce's arm and slid a needle into a vein near the crook of his elbow. 'I suspect that you're dehydrated. That's why I'm checking your bloods.'

Bruce wrinkled his nose. 'But dehydration is nothing. It shouldn't make me feel like this.'

She finished drawing the blood and pressed a cotton ball against his skin. 'Dehydration can cause a heart arrhythmia called atrial fibrillation. I think that's what's happened to you. It's an electrical disorder affecting the upper chambers of the heart, which means it's not pumping as regularly as it should. Did you feel anything strange?'

He gave a slow nod. 'I felt I had palpitations for a minute or so. But it wasn't sore. There was no pain.'

She put her hand on his arm and pointed to the monitor. 'Dehydration can cause atrial fibrillation. There can be a few other things, which we can rule out with some tests. Your heart rate seems to have gone back to normal now, but I'd like to keep an eye on you for another hour or so.'

He gave a little sigh and leaned back against the pillow. 'Will you let my boss know where I am?'

She gave him a nod and a smile. 'I will, and, Bruce? I think you need to find another training partner. Austin Mitchell might be a bit too serious for you. I'm just about to give him a new training plan and I don't think he'll be happy.'

Bruce leaned back against the pillows and closed his eyes, a smile painted across his face. 'May the force be with you.'

'What?'

Austin stared at the colour-coded programme in front of him. Usually he liked timetables. Usually he liked training plans. This one he didn't like one bit.

He held up the piece of paper. 'Is this a joke?'

Dr Carter stared up at him with those big green eyes of hers. She was sitting behind her desk. It was almost as if she were trying to ensure he knew who was in charge here. 'Why would you think it's a joke, Lieutenant Commander Mitchell?'

She had that clipped tone in her voice. The one she used when she was being the boss. Sometimes he liked it, but today it was like a red rag to a bull.

She was using his proper title. Other candidates got called by their first names. She'd hardly ever said his first name out loud. It was almost as if she were trying to force a distance between them.

The piece of paper started to crumple in his hand. 'I have my own training regime.'

'Not any more.' She stood up and folded her arms across her chest.

'Excuse me?' He was getting irritated now. Irritated because as soon as she'd stood up he'd caught a glimpse of those shapely legs and they were distracting him.

She walked around the desk towards him and took the crumpled paper from his hand. 'I'm in charge of all candidates' training plans. Think of it as a prescription.'

He pointed to the plan. 'But that's kids' play.'

He saw the little flicker next to her jaw. She was mad. But right now he didn't care. He was religious about his exercise regime. He didn't want anyone interfering with it.

She reached over and prodded his bicep. 'Your training programme has been specially formulated. We need all our candidates to be fit. We usually recommend one hour of cardio and one hour of resistance training every day. But you have more muscle bulk than the rest of the candidates.' She stared at him hard. 'You must realise that muscle wastage is one of the biggest problems for our astronauts.' For the first time today a smile hinted at her lips. 'If your muscles are overdeveloped you'll suffer from more muscle wastage in space. You'll be up in space, Lieutenant Commander, where will all that lactic acid go?'

Boy, she was cute when she flirted. But he wasn't going to get distracted.

'I'm already in top shape. This programme will bring me down. Why would anyone want to do that?'

'Because this isn't just about you. If you stay in your current shape your muscles will atrophy quicker than everyone else's and you'll feel the effects. It will affect your performance on the team.'

Boy, she was good. She seemed to know exactly what to say to stop him arguing. And she wasn't finished. 'You do a lot of weight training, don't you? And you probably take those protein drinks too? We'll need to have a look at that to check if that's really the best for you. This is all about forward planning, you know. Space is the ultimate goal. It's my job to make sure you'll be fit enough to take all the effects a no-gravity environment will throw at you.' She took the crumpled sheet and smoothed it back out on her desk, then pushed it back across to him. 'So, let me do my job. Follow my instructions.'

She was back to her no-nonsense approach. He stood for a few seconds, letting her aroma of scrubbed-clean soap and light floral perfume drift around him. She was wearing a pale yellow shirt with some kind of print on it. It was tucked tightly into her skirt, but he was imagining it knotted at that slim waist of hers along with a very hot pair of denim shorts. Now, that would be perfect.

'Lieutenant?' She was looking at him suspiciously, as if she'd just guessed exactly what was going through his mind.

He shot her a smile. 'You're right,' he said as he took the plan from her hand, brushing his fingers against hers. 'Space is the ultimate goal.' He headed towards the door and spun back round just before he left. 'As for the plan…' he waved it at her '… I'll let you know.'

He laughed as her chin dropped but didn't wait for her response. He had other plans for that.

# CHAPTER SIX

IT WAS THE most chilled she'd felt in a week. Things had settled down a bit. Austin Mitchell wasn't there every time she turned around. Her stomach had stopped doing flip-flops and had reduced itself to a steady buzz.

Her senses had stopped being in a state of overdrive. The skin on her fingers had finally stopped tingling and she'd stopped licking her lips whenever he was around.

The rest of the team had finally finished with the quips. Because there wasn't anything to quip about. Really.

She didn't lie in her bed at night and think about Austin Mitchell. He didn't cross her mind at all on the drive to work in the morning. And now, her favourite part of the evening, sitting on her porch on her rocker drinking a glass of wine, he definitely didn't feature on her radar.

She rested her feet up on the white railing and looked out onto the fields beyond. The old farmhouse was her dream come true; she might not own all the land around it, but at least she had the pleasure of the view of rolling fields.

She rested her head back and sipped her wine. There was a tiny speck in the distance. She watched carefully. The farmer and his workers were rarely around at this time of night—and if they were, they were usually in some kind of tractor.

She kept her eyes on the figure. It wasn't as if there were anything else to do. Her book was lying on the deck and she wasn't a big fan of TV.

She took another sip of her wine. It was definitely a guy and he was running at some pace. She frowned. This was a good way off the beaten track. Who on earth would be running out here?

Her heart rate quickened a little. The runner was definitely heading in this direction. She wasn't exactly dressed for guests. As soon as she got home from work the power suits were back on their hangers and she pulled on whatever she could find. Today's wardrobe was an old pale pink T-shirt and even older skimpy pink shorts. Perfect for being home alone. Not so perfect for giving some lost runner directions.

She pulled her feet down from the railing and leaned forward. Her eyes narrowed. Something about this runner was looking vaguely familiar. If he had a T-shirt it had disappeared. All she could see was the defined muscles on his chest and sculpted legs. Something prickled down her spine.

No way. *No way.*

But yes. The short dark hair and tall frame were definitely familiar. The biceps were even more familiar. She picked up her wine glass again and took a quick slug. What on earth was he doing out here?

A tiny part of her brain tried to be rational. Maybe he was just out for a run and he'd got lost? This could all be some crazy kind of fate-ridden coincidence.

Her body was flushed with heat. But she couldn't make a single bit of sense of her thoughts. Was she angry? Curious? Or secretly delighted?

He was getting closer. She could see the confident expression on his face. The smile was already there. Oh, this was definitely planned. Austin Mitchell didn't get lost.

She took a deep breath and stood up, trying her best to act cool, leaning on the railing and holding her wine glass in her hands as he slowed down.

His whole body was glistening with sweat in the early evening sun. He pulled his T-shirt from its hiding place at the back of his shorts and wiped his face. His breathing was laboured. He hadn't sneakily parked his car somewhere—from what she knew of Lieutenant Commander Mitchell he'd probably run from the actual base.

She gave him a cool smile. 'You seem to be lost, Lieutenant Commander Mitchell.'

He looked around at her clapboard house. Was he searching for a husband? Kids? No. He would have done his homework before he showed up at her door. He probably was secure in the knowledge that no one had quite met up to her exacting standards so far.

He was still breathing heavily. The cheeky grin was firmly in place. 'So it seems. Nice place you got here.'

Darn it. That rich drawl sent a wave of shivery delight down her spine. 'I like it,' she answered simply, doing her best to look cool even though every tiny hair on her skin was currently standing on end.

He placed his hands on his hips and just kept staring at her. She was feeling a little self-conscious. The T-shirt was old enough to be a size too small, pulled tight across her breasts. The shorts? Could probably do with her tugging them back down. But she refused to be intimidated by him—even though he was standing in front of her with his perfectly sculpted chest resembling some kind of Greek god. She bit the inside of her cheek, trying to remember why she'd told him he had to lose some muscle.

'I didn't tell you where I live.'

His comeback was just as quick. 'I didn't ask.'

Now, she couldn't help but start to smile. It seemed to be infectious whenever this guy was around. The cheek just radiated from him a mile high. On occasion she could be annoyed by it. But out of the WSSA environment things were a little different. She wasn't assessing him right now. She wasn't instructing him—not yet, anyway.

Her eyes swept the landscape. There wasn't another person around for miles. It was part of the reason she stayed here. It meant that the possibilities were endless.

She bent over, picked up her wine and topped up her glass, laughing as she did so. She could practically feel his eyes searing into her backside. 'So, it's pure misfortune that you've just happened to run miles into the countryside and land at my door?'

He gave her the kind of smile that could make any WSSA rocket take off on its own. 'Maybe it's coincidence?'

She raised her eyebrows and held up her glass towards him. 'Do you want me to estimate the probability stats for you of running randomly from the base—in any direction—for any distance and landing at my door?'

He took a step forward and leaned against her railing. 'I guess it's just lucky I found you, then. Call it a homing beacon.'

She couldn't hide the shiver down her spine. The flirting was getting out of hand. But not one single part of her wanted to stop it. His scent drifted over in the evening air. Sweat, testosterone, remnants of antiperspirant. All just aromas of him. It was almost hypnotic. And it absolutely was having a direct effect on her senses. The air between them was pheromone city.

This would be on her terms. Her choice. And as long as he understood that, things would be fine.

She leaned down over the railing towards him. There

was something kind of nice about being above the guy who normally towered over you. 'So, Austin, what did you plan to do when you got here?'

He glanced around him. It was obvious he was making sure there was no one else around. No one to disturb them. The anticipation of what might come next made her tingle all over.

He tugged at his shorts. 'I was thinking I could take a shower.'

She threw back her head and laughed at the bare-faced cheek of him. 'I'm sure you have an excellent shower at home, Lieutenant Commander Mitchell. You didn't need to run all this way to use mine.' She turned to walk away but he was too quick. He jumped up on the outside of her railing and grabbed her arm.

'So, it's back to Lieutenant Commander Mitchell, is it? A few seconds ago I was Austin.'

Her heart started thudding against her chest. She didn't have time to look down at where his hand was on her skin. Her whole body was too busy reacting to his touch. A little war had started somewhere in her stomach and she had no idea who was currently winning.

She couldn't look at his hand because his face was only inches from hers. Now, they were straight on. She wasn't looking up at him. She was looking straight at him. Straight into his eyes. Just as he was looking at hers.

Up close and personal was so different. Up close and personal away from the base was even more different. There was no one watching. No one to comment. No one to say anything. Just him. And her.

He was smiling again with those film-star straight white teeth. She could see a few tiny wrinkles around his eyes and some cute freckles across the bridge of his nose. All the parts of his skin she could see were lightly tanned.

The palm of her hand itched to reach out and touch his chest. To feel his muscles under her hands. A tiny trickle of sweat slid down from his forehead.

He was still smiling at her. Waiting. As if he knew what would happen next. As if he was letting her give the sign of what would come next.

It was unconscious. She couldn't help it. But her tongue slid across her lips. His eyes darted to her lips and she held her breath.

'Maybe it could be Austin again,' she whispered.

He leaned forward. 'Maybe it could.' He gave her his trademark sexy smile. The one guaranteed to have a hundred teenage girls swooning when he became an astronaut. There was no doubt. Not a second's hesitation as his lips captured hers. His hand caught the back of her head, tangling through her soft hair and anchoring her in position. Not that she'd want to be anywhere else.

Her hands slid across his shoulders. She could feel his muscles quivering under her touch, and the sheen on his skin, still slightly damp. She inhaled deeply and all she could smell was…*him*.

He was like a drug. There was nothing sensitive and sweet about this kiss. Austin Mitchell *knew* how to kiss a girl.

His lips were all over hers. His teeth brushing against them, his tongue probing into her mouth. Teasing. Tantalising. Making her think illicit thoughts.

A mixture of pheromones and adrenaline was coursing through her body. It was addictive. She could *so* get used to this. So get used to the feel of his body next to hers.

He leaned her back just a little, moving away from her mouth and concentrating on the delicate skin around her neck and behind her ears. For the first time in her life she actually felt her knees tremble. It was like being a teenager all over again and dreaming about kissing that movie star from the latest film. Except she wasn't dreaming. She was living the whole experience.

And it was even better than she could have imagined.

His hands started to move. Leaving the back of her head and tracing little lines down her back and round to her hips. One moved lower, touching the bare skin at the back of her thigh, hovering around the edge of her shorts.

She pressed a little closer. It was awkward. There was a railing directly between them both. She didn't know whether to be happy or sad. She wasn't quite sure how far she wanted this to progress. Her body might be acting one way but her brain was definitely holding a little in reserve.

He was a candidate. There might not be official rules about them dating but she was sure it wouldn't go down well.

His hand swept around towards her stomach and she sucked in a breath and laughed. It was automatic. He laughed too and pulled his lips apart from hers, pressing their foreheads together.

It gave her a few seconds to catch her breath.

His fingers tickled around her belly button. For a minute she wondered if they were going to make an attempt to go lower. His other hand was now cradling her bum. If there hadn't been a railing between them she would have been able to feel every inch of his body against hers.

And the more she thought about that—the more she craved it.

His fingers moved along her bare skin, skirting upwards towards her breasts. It was like butterfly wings dancing against her skin. They hit the jackpot. Cupping her breast and playing with her hardened nipple. A wave of sensations swept over her body and she let out an involuntary moan.

It was like a firework going off in her brain.

Her body took a step back, her forehead still connected with his. She sneaked her hand under her T-shirt and closed it over his, gently pulling it down and out, resting it on her hipbone.

He didn't object, didn't make any attempt to persuade her to change her mind. And somehow she knew, deep down, that he wouldn't. That made him almost perfect.

'This could get complicated,' she whispered, her breath ragged.

He smiled. 'Yes. It could.'

After a few seconds he leaned back, then jumped down from the railing, standing on the ground beneath her. He grabbed his T-shirt and pulled it over his head.

The confidence was still there. He still had that assuredness that drove her crazy.

She didn't want to admit what it did to other parts of her system.

He gave her a wink. 'We'll talk exercise programmes some other time, Dr Carter. In the meantime, let's see if we can come to a compromise about another kind of exercise.'

The implication was loud and clear. She couldn't have expected anything less—but he still shocked her.

She shook her head as he started off running again, moving quickly across the ground in the direction he'd come.

Her legs had gone all spongy and she half staggered back against the wall of the house, one hand across her belly, the other up next to her throat.

The skin that he'd touched was still tingling. It was on fire. Craving his touch again.

No one had ever kissed her like that. Ever.

She fixed on his figure as he disappeared into the distance, pressing her lips together to stop her calling him back.

Austin Mitchell was bad news.

Very bad news.
And she would have to keep telling herself that.
Over and over again.

# CHAPTER SEVEN

CORRINE STARED AT the records in front of her. She had the oddest feeling.

She stood up and walked over to her glass window. The candidates were on the other side of it, in the computer tech room learning about some of the equipment on the space station.

It didn't matter how hard she tried. Her eyes went first to Austin. He was talking to Lisa Kravitz, the school teacher. They were laughing and joking as they tried to repair something wearing the biggest pair of gloves imaginable. They would do the same exercise over and over again in the next few months, eventually trying it in a zero-gravity environment. Lisa threw back her head and laughed at something Austin had said.

Corrine felt a little surge of jealousy but shook it off immediately. She'd spent the last two weeks avoiding Austin. It hadn't been too hard. The candidates had spent most of the last two weeks in lectures and learning from manuals. People really had no idea how much equipment was in use in space, and how many things could go wrong with it. Every member of the team had to be able to maintain, repair and rebuild essential equipment if necessary. It wasn't easy to find spare parts in space and they often had to improvise.

In any case, whenever she closed her eyes her brain went into overtime. It was almost as if the memory of that kiss was haunting her. To say nothing of the buzz that flared in her skin or her lips.

The last thing she wanted to do right now was to be face to face with Austin Mitchell.

But Lisa Kravitz was another story. She folded her arms across her chest. The candidates were monitored regularly and Lisa had lost a little weight. She looked tired. It could just be that she was excited about her training and was eating differently from normal. But was she also looking a little paler?

Some people didn't believe in gut instinct. But in Corrine's experience it had always served her well.

It was time to call Lisa in for some blood work. As she moved away Austin looked up and caught her eye. This time there was no smile. No wink.

Instead, for the first time since she'd met him, he put his head down and carried on with his work.

Darn it. One glimpse of familiar dark suit was enough to distract him from the task at hand. His screwdriver slipped from his hand and landed on the mat below. Opposite him, Lisa gave the air a punch. 'Yes, I win!'

He grimaced. He hated losing—at anything. This was no different.

But what smarted even more was the fact that he hadn't even caught Corrine Carter looking.

By the time he'd run the six miles back to camp after that kiss his body still hadn't returned to normal. He'd had to stand in the coldest shower known to man to try and still the blood pumping around his body.

This was driving him nuts. From the moment he'd heard those heels clicking across the hangar towards him and

Corrine Carter had come into view every sense in his body had been on fire.

This wasn't him. This wasn't the kind of person he was.

He couldn't be. He had a goal. Space. And he'd long ago realised that to get there everything else had to be sidelined.

He'd excelled as a navy pilot. He'd been top of his class when he'd studied microbiology. He'd loved the job as a Top Gun instructor. But it had all just been part of the bigger plan. The one that took him to the ultimate goal.

And he'd seen many colleagues fall by the wayside. Serious relationships were off the cards. Sure, he dated—but never for too long. A few months tops. He couldn't afford the distractions. He'd seen other pilots and RIO's affected by months away from their partners and children. One of his good friends had blown a test flight after finding out his kid was away for emergency surgery. It had taken two days to find him in the Arizona desert. All because he hadn't been focused on the job. And that was what was driving Austin nuts.

He closed his eyes at night and images of Corrine Carter danced around his brain. The way her skirt hugged the curves of her backside. The way he permanently wanted to pull her shirts from her waistband. The fact that those long shapely legs and killer heels always caught his eye. It didn't matter that she was always dressed appropriately and slightly demurely. The thing that was killing him was that he wanted to know what lay beneath.

The flirtation was obvious. She was attracted to him. He was attracted to her.

But she had reservations about acting on it. Whereas he had none at all.

Because he needed to get Corrine Carter out of his system.

The other night had been pure impulse. He'd been about

two minutes into his run when he'd decided exactly where to go. The sight of Corrine in her skimpy T-shirt and shorts had made him realise he'd done exactly the right thing. Seeing her sitting in her old rocker on her wraparound porch, sipping wine, had almost made him think that she'd been waiting for him.

He was surprised when he'd checked out her address. He'd expected her to stay in some serviced apartment on the outskirts of the city. The pale yellow clapboard farmhouse had been more than a little surprising. He only wished he'd got to see the inside.

It seemed odd. Corrine was a stunner, with her own place and a great job. He was more than a little surprised that some guy hadn't completely swept her off her feet already. But there was something there. Something a little different. At times, she could seem a little detached. As if there were an invisible barrier just in front of her that stopped anyone getting too close. Why would she be like that?

He frowned and picked up his screwdriver from the floor. Lisa was still bouncing around the place. He fixed her with a stare. She'd been good company since the start of training and they often joked together.

'Right, lady. First time was a fluke. Ready for a rematch?'

She spun around and put her hands on her hips. 'Totally. But if I win again you have to go and find me a chocolate-frosted, custard-filled doughnut.'

He raised his eyebrows. 'Interesting choice. Very specific.'

She put her arms back in the oversized gloves. 'I know what I like.'

He nodded in approval. 'Do I get to tell the doc about your diet choices?'

She gave him a quick wink. 'Oh, I'm sure you and the doc can come to an understanding about what's kept secret.' She had a dopey smile on her face.

He narrowed his gaze. Other people were definitely noticing. And that was partly his fault after the dare in the bar. They thought it had something to do with his love of a challenge rather than anything else. More distractions.

He *had* to get this woman out from under his skin.

Lisa gave a little cough. 'Darn it. Trust me to get an itch while I'm stuck in these gloves.'

Austin decided to be wicked. 'Want me to scratch it for you?'

Lisa laughed. 'Not a chance, buster. You know I'm going to beat you. You're just running scared.'

He gave his best villain impersonation. 'Prepare to be annihilated.'

Lisa laughed again in response. 'Game on.'

The next day Austin snaked his way through the streets until he finally found what he was looking for. He wasn't familiar with Clear Lake City and he'd asked a few colleagues for recommendations. Tomorrow they were due to test the T-38 planes to continue part of their training. Tonight, he wanted the best burger in town and this was apparently the place.

He pushed open the door. Retro was in. The sixties-style diner didn't look as if it had changed one bit. The waitresses wore sticky-out dresses with little hats on their heads and the place was filled with traditional red leather booths and a whole range of bar stools along the counter.

One of the waitresses appeared at his arm. 'Just the one?'

He nodded. He'd had a few other things to pick up in the city before his trip so had come in on his own.

She lifted a menu and walked over, gesturing towards a table. He slid into the booth with a smile. She acknowledged him with a nod. 'You've made it just in time. We're expecting the city tour to stop here any minute—but don't worry, I'll take your order first. Coffee?'

He shook his head. 'Just a diet cola right now, thanks.'

The door behind him opened and around thirty people filed in. He had made it just in time. The waitresses wasted no time in seating everyone, filling the diner to capacity.

He jerked when he recognised the person at the back of the queue. Corrine.

He had to look twice. She wasn't wearing her traditional dark suit—or those cute funky shorts. She had on a red wraparound dress and black wedge sandals. It was the first time he'd ever seen her in red and, boy, did she suit it.

He gestured to the waitress. 'Tell the young lady she's welcome to share my booth.'

The waitress gave a knowing smile. 'I'll do just that.'

She walked across the diner and put her hand on Corrine's arm, pointing towards the booth. Her eyes widened in shock before she pulled herself together and walked towards him.

She slid into the seat opposite and rolled her eyes. 'Fancy seeing you here.'

'What? I asked someone for a recommendation for the best burger in Clear Lake. They sent me here.'

She shook her head and laughed. 'So, it's just some weird coincidence, then.' She narrowed her gaze. 'Who did you ask?'

'Blair King.'

Now she really did laugh. Blair King was one of Corrine's fellow instructors. 'I'll be having words with Blair. He knows that this is my favourite place to eat. He'd better not be doing what I think he's doing.'

Austin leaned across the table towards her. 'And what might that be?'

'Annoy me,' she said quickly as she picked up the menu, then set it back down again.

'Go on, then,' he said. 'If you eat here all the time, what should I order?' What was wrong with him? So much for putting distance between them and having no distractions. He only had to be in her vicinity before he automatically started flirting with her. He just couldn't help it. And that probably annoyed him the most.

She leaned her head on her hand. 'Well, that depends. Are you here for a main course or a dessert?'

'Definitely a main course.' *And I'd prefer it if that was you.* She'd slipped off her jacket and his eyes were naturally drawn to the tiny hint of cleavage on display in the wrap dress. It was a softer look than she normally wore. More comfortable-looking. With a definite hint of sexy.

She looked down at the menu, running her finger down the plastic coating. Fingers that had touched him. Fingers that had skimmed over the skin on his back and shoulders and then settled somewhere just north of his waistline. Just a pity they'd been at the back and not the front.

She tilted her head to the side and tucked some hair behind her ear, revealing the soft skin around her neck and décolletage. She looked up and met his gaze. 'I think you're a megaburger kind of guy. With maybe a dash of piri-piri sauce.'

He gave a thoughtful nod. 'Really?' He glanced over at the menu. 'You could be right. So, what's your poison going to be?'

She pointed to the countertop where a variety of cakes sat under glass domes. 'I'm going to have a piece of the Thundertop cake.'

'Thundertop cake? What on earth is that?'

She smiled. 'It's vanilla sponge, with a dash of orange, sandwiched with raspberry jam and coconut and marshmallow frosting.'

He shuddered. 'Ugh. No way.'

'What's wrong? You not a dessert kind of guy?'

Why was it that a seemingly innocent question seemed so different when it came from her lips? He pushed aside all the illicit thoughts that sprang to mind, of what he could do with dessert and Corrine Carter.

'Depends on the circumstances,' he said quickly, before giving her a sly smile, 'And, of course, who I'm with.'

She shook her head and sat back as the waitress came and took their order.

'You're quite the flirt, aren't you, Austin Mitchell?'

He leaned closer. 'Like I said, depends who I'm with.'

He couldn't help it. He knew his confidence wound her up. She didn't need to know he didn't always feel completely comfortable. It was just the best face for the world he was in. No one wanted an unsure pilot flying their aircraft—or, worse, spacecraft.

She tapped her nails on the table. 'So you think it's okay to flirt with one of your instructors?'

'I haven't seen any rules against it.'

She allowed a tiny nod in agreement. 'But you think it's okay to turn up at someone's house uninvited and practically pin them to their wall and kiss them?'

He leaned back against the leather booth. 'I didn't exactly pin you to the wall. But that could be arranged if you want.'

She waved her hand. 'You don't even know me. You don't know the first thing about me. Nor I you.' She wagged her finger at him. 'So, you certainly shouldn't be kissing me.'

'Maybe you should have objected?' He liked this. He

liked the way they batted back and forward between each other. He liked that she gave as good as she got. He liked it even better when he found a way to push her buttons.

She shifted in her seat, giving him a better view of her cleavage. 'Next time, maybe I will.'

'Who says there'll be a next time?'

She looked him straight in the eye as the waitress set down their drinks. 'I do.'

Had she really just said that? Was she out of her tiny mind?

What was it about being away from the base? While she was at work, it was easy to put everything in boxes and keep Austin Mitchell at a distance.

She had never been like this. *Never.* This guy made her hormones surge around her body to the point where they affected her mind, her mouth and her actions. There must be some science behind this.

But at the end of the day the science didn't matter. Because Austin Mitchell had that look on his face. The sexy, knowing smile. Knowing exactly how much he affected her.

Maybe it was the fact he wasn't in uniform? While the bright blue flight suit did crazy things to his eyes, it always made her remember the distance between them. Today, in dark blue jeans and a short-sleeved white shirt, Austin Mitchell could be any regular guy on the planet.

If regular guys looked this good.

The waitress appeared again and took their order. Austin was still watching her with those hypnotic blue eyes of his. She wasn't going to look at them. She just wasn't. It was too much trouble.

She sucked in a breath and tried to bring some normality back to the situation. 'I'm not used to being kissed by guys I hardly know. Why don't we try and remedy that situation?' She gulped. That had come out a little more direct than intended. It was almost an invitation to tell her a little about him and see what could happen next.

She twisted her feet under the table. He couldn't see her squirm there.

Austin sat back a little. He just looked amused by everything she said. 'You've read my file. What else do you want to know?'

She shook her head. 'I've read your medical file. I haven't read your general file. I had no need to. So, unless we want to discuss your blood work, eye tests or chest X-ray, I really don't know much about you at all.'

He leaned back against the leather seat. 'You know I was a Top Gun instructor.'

'And that's all that defines you? A Top Gun instructor?'

'It's enough for most women.'

She shook her head. 'Why did you join the navy? Why be a pilot?'

He looked a little more thoughtful, and his answers were more measured. He spoke slowly. 'Let's just say it's a family tradition.'

Now, she was finding out a bit more. 'Your dad was a pilot?'

He nodded. 'My father, my grandfather and my great-grandfather.'

'Wow.' She paused for a second. There was something a little strange about the way he said it. 'So, Top Gun wasn't your dream?'

His eyes darted off to the side. She smiled. He was formulating an answer.

'Yes…and no.'

She tapped her fingers on the table. 'Now, what does that mean?'

He met her gaze with such an intensity she caught her

breath. 'Space. Space has always been the dream. I knew that one of the best ways in was to be a pilot. That's why I was happy to follow the family tradition.' He paused for a second. 'My father was on the shortlist for astronaut training thirty-five years ago. Then along came a baby that gave him scarlet fever and then measles and those plans went out the window.'

'Wow, talk about a guilt trip.'

He shrugged. 'What can I say? My father was never a baby kind of guy. First proper conversation we had was when I told him I was joining the navy and planned on being a pilot.'

'He approved?'

'You could say that. He spends his life telling the world how well his son is doing. As for this?' He held up his hands. 'On the one hand he can't wait to tell folks his son is an astronaut candidate, and on the other...' His voice tailed off a little. 'I think he still feels a little bitter about missing out on the opportunity himself. He asks detailed questions about some of the assignments, then proceeds to tell me how he could have completed it easier and faster than me.'

She sucked in some air. 'So, you're treading a fine line between fatherly approval and fatherly jealousy?'

He gave a wry smile. 'Maybe. But some things I get to keep to myself.' He met her gaze. 'If it's not astronaut or Top Gun he's really not interested.'

*But she was.*

She leaned across the table towards him. Austin Mitchell was getting a whole lot more interesting.

'So what are you keeping to yourself, Lieutenant Commander Mitchell?'

She wanted to laugh out loud. She was blatantly flirting with the guy. But he made it so easy.

He raised his eyebrows, then leaned across the table towards her too, their faces only inches apart, and waved his hand. 'Space has always been the goal. But there's more than one way to get there. I loved science at school. If I wanted to go to space, I should really have focused on physics. But it was biology I loved—microbiology. Things down at a cellular level. Plants, animals and humans, but mainly just the science.'

She smiled. 'So, that's why you did your degree too?'

He nodded. 'It made sense.' He gave her a cheeky smile. 'Men aren't supposed to like multitasking, but I did.' It was a quip about her remark at the pool that day and she couldn't help but smile. 'Astronauts are selected today not just because they have one skill. I decided to give myself the best chance of selection, increase my chances.'

'So you can pilot the craft *and* do the on-board experiments?'

'Exactly.'

Interesting. This guy had been absolutely determined to go to space. She couldn't even begin to think about what he would have done if he hadn't been selected.

The waitress appeared and set down their order. Corrine didn't wait. She picked up her fork and took her first taste of the cake she loved. It looked kind of odd. Austin with his megaburger and her with a piece of cake.

'What about you?'

She looked up. She shouldn't be surprised. It was only fair. She'd asked him some questions, so he had to be allowed to do the same.

'What about me?'

'Why are you at WSSA?'

She smiled. 'I guess we're not that dissimilar. I always wanted to work at WSSA.' She pointed to the sky. 'But I never dreamed of going into space. I always wanted my feet to stay firmly on the ground.'

'Why WSSA?'

She took a few seconds. 'Because it's where dreams are made. The science of sending someone into space is fascinating. There's still so much we don't know—and can still find out. Wouldn't you like to think that there's life on another planet somewhere?'

He looked surprised. 'You believe in aliens?'

She laughed. 'Absolutely. They're green with big heads.' She shook her head. 'No, seriously. I have mixed feelings about all that. I know, statistically, with the size of our universe, it's possible. Do I really think there's something out there? I just don't know.'

Now she was curious. Astronauts could be divided on this. 'What about you?'

He shook his head. 'I'm more of a believer of the fact that we've done serious damage to our planet and in future years we might need to live in space—or somewhere else.'

She sat back a little. 'You think you'll end up living in space?'

He shook his head. 'Not me. But our children. Our future generations.'

There was just something about the way he said those words. The way he looked at her as he said them. *Our children.* She knew he didn't mean it that way. But her body didn't seem to understand that. Every tiny hair she had was currently standing on end and her mouth had gone inexplicably dry.

He didn't seem to notice the effect his words had on her. He was on a roll. 'I was probably born five hundred years too early. I really want to be living in the time of space travel that we see on TV and in movies, with all their technology. But hopefully I'm going to help us get there.'

She smiled. Lots of the astronauts had been inspired by TV series. Particularly the science. 'I'd be really grateful if you could make me a Tricorder. Just think, I point something at your body, scan and it tells me exactly what's wrong with you. Think how brilliant that would be.'

He shook his head. 'Get in line. I'll only make you a Tricorder once I've developed the transporter. I want to press a button and beam to another planet.'

She laughed. 'You want all your cells reduced to atoms and molecules and scattered throughout space?'

'Only if we can put them back together in the same order.' He gave her a wicked look. 'I'd hate to find some parts of my anatomy missing...' he raised his eyebrows '...or find any part of you misplaced.'

She shuddered. 'I can't even think about that.' She sighed. 'I'd just love to be able to study the science of sending humans to Mars. Long-term missions. That kind of thing.' She stared off into the sky for a few seconds. 'But it's kind of scary. Especially if the journey is only one-way.' She looked back at him. He was watching her with a strange expression on his face. 'Would you sign up for something like that?'

He took a few seconds to answer. 'I might,' he said carefully. 'That kind of journey is going to be inevitable at some point. Every astronaut will have to ask themselves that question. I guess it all depends on what they leave behind.'

He couldn't possibly realise how cold those words sounded to her. How alone. She didn't even want to have this kind of conversation with Austin Mitchell. When he was in front of her all she really wanted to think about was the here and now. Not the future. Especially when the aloneness of it sent a shiver down her spine. She decided to change the subject.

She nodded at his megaburger. 'I hope you know I'm secretly keeping note of your eating habits.'

'I hope you remember that you recommended it.' He smiled. Mars forgotten.

'Smart answer.'

He gave her a careful glance. 'That's a nice house you've got. Kinda big for one person.'

'What are you asking me?'

'You know exactly what I'm asking you.' He was getting straight back to point. Seemed as if his mind was on the here and now too.

'Lieutenant Commander Mitchell, I'm shocked. You kissed a girl without finding out her availability?'

He raised one eyebrow. 'I kissed a girl based on the chemistry between us.'

She gulped. Talk about getting straight to the point. 'You can't just go around kissing people.'

'You can't just go around kissing people back.'

Every time she tried to push him back in his box he jumped straight back out. The sizzle in the air between them was practically causing sparks.

His fingers were just across the table from hers. If she inched her fingers forward just a little, they would touch. But where would that lead?

Nowhere good.

'You did kiss me back—remember?'

The Texas drawl was rich and thick. Like melted chocolate dripping all over her skin. For a few seconds she couldn't breathe. This guy had a ridiculous effect on her. Maybe she would be better to try and get him out of her system?

*Where had that come from?*

That wasn't like her at all. She didn't do things like that. She didn't think things like that. What was it about this guy that was making her brain scramble whenever he was around?

It was driving her crazy. She'd never had one of these lightning-bolt attractions. A 'fireworks going off in the background whenever he was around' kind of thing.

She licked her lips as her eyes fixed on the table. 'I might have kissed you back,' she said quietly.

His fingers moved, stretching across to touch hers.

The effect was instant. Her eyes met his. 'Wanna kiss me back again?'

He couldn't have been more direct.

And it lit a fire under her like never before.

She hadn't even answered before he turned to the waitress and lifted his hand. 'Can we get the check, please?'

The next few moments passed in a blur. Austin glanced at the check and left a pile of dollars on the table. He was on his feet in an instant, holding his hand out towards her.

She hesitated.

'Shall we?'

She was doing her best to appear calm. To calm the racing heart in her chest and the buzzing in her ears. The jumbled thoughts swirling around her mind stilled, giving her one clear thought and one clear answer.

She slid along the booth and reached her hand out to his.

It was the weirdest thing. But she'd never had a clearer thought in her head.

She was going to do this.

For the first time in her life. She was going to be bad.

# CHAPTER EIGHT

HE MUST BE losing his mind. But right now, Austin Mitchell could only focus on one thing—and for about the first time in twenty years it wasn't on getting to space.

They stood next to her car as she fumbled with her keys. He was pretty sure this was completely out of character for Corrine Carter. Even though she was trying to be confident and determined he could see the tiny flare of panic in her eyes.

He walked around to the driver's side of the car and put his hand over hers. 'Do you want me to drive?'

She nodded without speaking, handed him the keys and disappeared to the other side of the car.

He climbed in, started the car and pulled out into the traffic. Neither of them spoke and the ten-mile journey seemed to take for ever. He was conscious of every tiny movement, every cross of her legs, the way she held her hands in her lap and the bounce of her hair on her shoulders.

His stomach was literally in knots the whole way. The last thing he wanted to happen was for Corrine to change her mind between the diner and the house.

The yellow clapboard house appeared in the distance. It was still a good-looking house, but now it seemed to represent so much more.

It was all he could do not to skid to a halt. Corrine jumped out of the car as soon as they stopped. Austin moved a little slower. The last thing he wanted to do was push her into doing something she didn't want to.

She unlocked the front door and turned to face him. 'Want to see inside?' It was supposed to be light. It was supposed to be fun. But he could hear the tiny wobble in her voice.

He kept his feet firmly planted on the porch and lifted his hand, running a finger down the side of her face. 'Corrine, do you know what you're doing?'

'No.' She blinked. The answer had come out automatically. She sucked in a deep breath and closed her hand around his. 'But I know I want to do it.'

She nudged her door with her hip, letting it swing open to reveal a wide hallway. 'You only get invited in once,' she said. This time she was smiling. This time, she seemed more confident, more relaxed.

He kept his voice low as he ran his finger along the length of her arm. 'In that case, I'd better say yes.'

Every part of her body was trembling. It was all she could do to stay on her feet. All she could smell was him. All she could see was him. Every word he spoke seemed to connect with the muscles in her legs and turn them to mush.

The expectation had been building too long. If she waited much longer she'd spontaneously combust and she had the distinct impression he'd do the same.

She grabbed his hand and pulled him along her hallway. A tiny wave of panic flared. Was her bedroom even tidy? When she'd left this morning she hadn't contemplated having a guest. That hadn't entered her head at all.

As they reached her bedroom door she turned around to face him. His reaction was instant; he captured her head in his hands and put his lips on hers. *This* was the kiss she remembered. But this time she could feel all his body against hers.

Now, she had every part of his muscle and sinew pressed up against her. This was the moment that had haunted her dreams for the last two weeks. And it felt even better than she'd imagined. One hand drifted down the side of her body, skimming her breast, her waistline and settling at her hip, where it tugged at the ties of her wrap dress.

She froze for a second.

'Hey, what's wrong?' he murmured in her ear.

She licked her lips. 'I just… I just…'

He put both hands on her hips and looked her square in the eye. 'You just, what?'

She gulped. One minute she'd been fine, the next she'd felt a tiny second of panic.

She was surprised he'd even noticed. But it felt good that he had.

'I like to be in control,' she said shakily.

He was watching her steadily. 'Corrine, did something happen?'

A little shiver coursed over her body. His gaze was intense. She could still feel the attraction buzzing in the air between them, but this needed to be on her terms. Her way.

'Let's just say I had a reason to learn self-defence.'

He flinched. Then reached over and touched her cheek. It was the gentlest touch. 'Did he hurt you?'

She squeezed her eyes closed for a second. This was not where she had wanted this to go. But she couldn't be truly comfortable with what was coming next if Austin didn't understand her.

She lifted her chin and swallowed, meeting his gaze. 'He tried to hurt me, so I hurt him back. I knocked him out.'

The corners of his lips turned upwards. 'That's my girl.'

He didn't say anything for a few seconds but just lifted his hand away from her cheek. 'Corrine, I will never do anything to hurt you. I won't even put a hand on you if you don't want me to. You can have all the control you want. And if you want me to leave, you just need to say.'

'No.' This time she did reach out. She put her hand on his arm. 'I don't want you to leave.'

'You're sure?' They might have flirted and joked together before, but right now there was absolute sincerity on Austin Mitchell's face.

And she believed it. He made her believe it.

'I'm sure.'

His eyes twinkled. 'Then let me ask you, Dr Carter, what do you want?'

Her fingers responded instantly, running up his chest and starting to undo the buttons on his white shirt. She hadn't even known her fingers could move that quickly. He didn't object. Not when she unfastened the last one and pushed the shirt back off his shoulders.

He took a tiny step closer. 'Hey, this is getting a little unfair.' His warm breath touched the skin at the bottom of her neck.

'Then make it fair,' she whispered. He gave her dress another tug, loosening the ties and letting the jersey material fall back and crumple to the floor.

She'd thought she'd feel self-conscious. It was hard not to around Austin. The guy didn't have a single muscle in his body that wasn't defined. But Austin seemed far more interested in her curves than how flat her stomach was.

His lips moved from hers, edging around the back of her ear and down to her throat. She released a little whimper and stepped backwards, pulling him with her towards the bed.

They hadn't stopped to turn on any lights, but the tiny

gap at the French doors made her white full-length gauze drapes flutter next to them. It was like a movie scene. All she needed was the smoke machine to finish setting the mood.

She felt safe. She felt safe with Austin.

Her hands moved towards his jeans. He lifted his head and closed his hand over hers. 'Last chance to change your mind, Corrine.'

She smiled. His voice was bathing her with a wave of sensations that she didn't ever want to end. She undid his belt buckle and pulled it sharply from his jeans, tossing it onto the floor.

His hand caressed her red bra as they fell back onto the white duvet laughing. 'I think we've passed the point of no return,' she said softly as she put her lips on his.

Austin woke up a few hours later, curled around the warm body of Corrine Carter. Her pale curtain was billowing in the wind again. The handyman in him wanted to offer to fix the draft around the door, but he knew that Corrine would refuse.

Something in his heart squeezed a little. This was the point where he should retrieve his clothes and head for the door. It wasn't as if he had any transport, but he'd run between the base and Corrine's house before and he could do it again.

But something felt weird. He didn't want to climb out of the bed and disappear. Even though he knew he had to.

He had to be focused for tomorrow. The T-38 super-sonic jet trainers were the start of his pilot training for piloting the spacecraft. It was a million-dollar programme. He had to be on point. No distractions. So why was he still here?

Corrine groaned and her warm body shifted back towards his. It was impossible. There was no way he could *not* react. After a few seconds she rolled over, smiling at him.

'Hey,' she said softly, her hand coming over and resting on his bare chest.

'Hey,' he replied, his hand connecting with her bare behind.

She was staring at him with those big green eyes. Up close and personal he could see tiny flecks of brown in them. Her skin was perfect, with only the tiniest hint of colour and not a single blemish. Her curves were even more perfect.

'I liked the red dress.' He smiled. 'You should wear it more often.'

'Seems to me you liked it better off than on,' she shot back.

His fingers trailed along her soft skin. 'Okay, you got me. I definitely liked it better off.'

'Austin...' Her voice tailed off. He sensed her muscles tense under the palms of his hands. This was it. This was the *don't-call-me-I'll-call-you* chat.

He'd never actually had anyone say that to him before. It had always been him doing it to someone else. He was usually the dumper rather than the dumped.

His stomach twisted uncomfortably.

She reached up and ran her fingers through his short hair, licking her lips as she did so. She was thinking of what to say. He could tell. She was trying to find just the right let-down words.

But then she surprised him.

'You could get addictive,' she with a sigh, then rolled onto her back and stared up at the ceiling.

Not what he was expecting and his heart did a little jig. It didn't matter that he'd decided he should get Corrine Carter out of his system. It didn't matter that he had no intention of starting any kind of relationship that interfered with his ultimate goal.

Those things didn't seem so crystal clear right now.

His phone beeped behind him.

'Who's that?'

He shook his head. 'I was waiting on an email. It must be that.'

He leaned out of the side of the bed and fumbled around his jeans, retrieving the phone from his pocket and pressing the button. It only took a few seconds to read the email.

'What is it?' She didn't bother to hide her curiosity.

Now it was his turn to sag back against the pillows. 'It's the offer of some research. It's been in the pipeline for a few years. It's just taken a long time to actually arrive.'

She leaned her head on her hand. 'What kind of research?'

'Cellular stuff. Looking at zebra fishes, in particular the Hedgehog signalling pathway and how it controls cell growth in human cancers.'

Her eyes widened. 'That sounds fascinating. And really worthwhile. They offered you the research?'

He nodded. 'They want me to head up the team. I did some preliminary research a few years ago and contributed to developing the theory they want to explore.'

'But what about WSSA?'

He didn't hesitate. 'WSSA comes first. It always will.'

There was a little flare of recognition behind her eyes. As if she understood he wasn't just talking about the research. He was talking about everything. His whole life.

'Will they give the project to someone else?'

He let out a long slow breath. He'd always known these two parts of his life could collide. He just hadn't expected it to be right now. 'Probably.'

'And you can't find any way to do both?'

He frowned. 'How on earth could I do that? I've got intensive training for the next eighteen months. I won't be able to think about anything else but that.' It came out a little sharper than he intended and she pulled the duvet closer to herself.

'You should speak to Jack Carson, who oversees things. There are all sorts of research projects done by WSSA. You don't know what they might be planning for the future.'

He shook his head. This conversation was making him uncomfortable. This was the first time—ever—he'd had reason to question going into space. This research was important. If they could find out how that pathway really worked and find a way to switch it off, it could affect every single person with cancer.

He swung his legs around out of the bed and picked up his jeans.

She didn't seem surprised—didn't do anything to stop him. He pulled on his jeans and walked over to get his shirt. She sat up too, pulling the duvet around her. 'Do you want me to drive you back to base?'

He shook his head. 'The walk will do me good. I've got a lot to think about. I need to work out how to turn them down.'

She gave a nod. 'You'll be on the other side of the base for the next few weeks. Good luck with the pilot training.'

His footsteps kind of faltered but he didn't turn around. He didn't let himself turn around. Last thing he needed right now was to see Corrine with her mussed-up hair, all wrapped up in a duvet, looking sexier than hell. He'd never be able to get that picture out of his head—whether he was on earth, or in space.

'Thanks,' he muttered quietly as he left, thinking about all the things he'd just done wrong.

# CHAPTER NINE

CORRINE STARED AT the blood results in front of her and felt numb.

She hated it when her gut instinct paid off. Particularly in this kind of way.

Lisa had abnormal blood counts. Nothing that could be diagnosed, but something that would require further investigations. She had a horrible feeling this was going to be out of her league.

There was a knock at the door and a pale-faced Lisa appeared.

'You wanted to see me.'

Corrine nodded. 'Take a seat,' she said, gesturing towards the seat beside her.

Lisa looked nervous. She was dressed in her blue flight suit and covered from head to toe, but even as she sat down she involuntarily scratched her arm.

'I just wondered how you're feeling. I have a few concerns. You look tired and you look as if you've lost a bit of weight. Would you mind if I weighed you today?'

'I've lost eleven pounds,' Lisa said quickly.

Corrine nodded. At this point, she would take Lisa's word for it. She needed to get to the bottom of things.

A tear started to trickle down Lisa's cheek. 'I just thought it was stress. I didn't want to talk to anyone about it, in case you thought I couldn't cope with the learning. This is my dream. I want this more than anything. I don't want to be the person who goes through all the interviews and tests and then can't cope with the workload.'

The words tumbled out, one after the other.

Corrine pressed her lips together. She was feeling guilty. If Lisa felt that she couldn't come and talk to her then she wasn't doing her job properly.

She slid an arm around Lisa's shoulder. 'I don't think this is stress. I don't think this has anything to do with your mental health. I think this is physical. Do you have any other symptoms you can tell me about?'

Lisa started scratching again. 'I'm itchy. I'm itchy all the time. I started taking antihistamines but they haven't helped at all. And I can't sleep at night. I keep sweating. It's driving me crazy. I kept thinking it's just because I'm in Texas and not used to the heat. Then I thought I must be stressed. I even had my husband send me my own pillow from home to see if that helped me sleep.'

'And it didn't?'

Lisa shook her head. Corrine took a deep breath. 'Lisa, would you mind if I examined you? I mean, all of you?'

Lisa's eyes widened at little. 'What did you find in the blood tests?'

Corrine kept her voice steady. 'Some of your blood levels were a little abnormal. But nothing that could be diagnosed at this point. I want to take a full history from you again and do a full examination. From there, we should be able to decide what other investigations you might need.'

Lisa nodded and stood up, reaching for the zip on her flight suit. 'But it will be something simple, won't it? Something you can treat easily?'

This was the hard bit. She didn't want to make false

promises. Not when she knew what was at stake. 'Let's wait and see.'

She was thorough. She was always thorough. Lisa was totally surprised when Corrine found raised lymph nodes in her groin and under her arm.

'What does that mean? Is it tumours?'

Corrine tried to answer carefully. 'Raised lymph nodes are normally the sign of some kind of infection. What I'd usually do is ask you to come back in two weeks to see if they were still there. But, because you've told me the other symptoms you've been having, I think it's best to refer you on to a specialist. They might do a fine needle biopsy to give them a better picture.'

'A fine needle biopsy where?'

Corrine spoke softly. 'Of one, or both, of the lymph nodes.'

Lisa sat up and zipped up her flight suit. 'I think I'm going to be sick.' Corrine made a grab for the trashcan.

*I think I'm going to be sick too.* Lisa had all the signs of non-Hodgkin lymphoma. It could only be diagnosed by a specialist. And it would be wrong for her to have that kind of discussion with Lisa now.

Lisa pulled her head up from the trashcan. 'This is it for me, isn't it?'

Everything inside Corrine's stomach twisted. Lisa should be talking about her life. But Corrine knew she was talking about her place on the programme. This was how they all were. All the candidates were so focused on completing the programme and getting into space that nothing else mattered. She got that.

She put a hand on Lisa's shoulder. 'Let's wait and see what the specialist says.'

'When will I get to see him?'

'Today. Let me make a few calls. I'll get someone to

see you and arrange transport. Do you want me to come with you?'

Lisa nodded numbly. 'I need to go. I need to take a few minutes.'

Corrine's heart squeezed for her. She'd just ripped this woman's hopes and dreams away in the blink of an eye. It was so cruel. Something that was totally out of her control. She'd become a doctor to help people. Not to tell them the thing they'd worked towards was now out of their grasp.

She leaned against her desk. She'd always loved her job. Like Lisa, she'd dreamed of it, worked hard for it and been delighted when she'd finally got it. How would she feel if someone ripped it away from her?

Her stomach turned over. Austin Mitchell.

Things had finished more than a little awkwardly the other day. She had to get it all into perspective.

If anyone found out they'd had intimate knowledge of each other…well, it wasn't against the rules. Lots of fellow colleagues had romanced, fallen in love and married. In a place this size with so many people, it wasn't that unusual.

But she didn't want to take any chances. She was responsible for Austin's medical assessments. She didn't want anyone to think she couldn't be impartial. She could fix this. She could. She'd swap with another medical colleague. That would keep everything above board and where it should be.

But she'd do it later.

Right now, she had to make a referral that could be devastating for a woman she liked and respected.

For the first time in her whole medical career, she hoped she was completely wrong.

The test flights had been exhilarating. He'd loved every second. It wasn't that everything came easy—there was always a lot to learn. It was just that he was a natural pilot. Within a few minutes he always had a feel of the plane and the controls, how light his touch needed to be. It was like being in tune with the machine—as if it were just an extension of yourself.

People who weren't pilots didn't get it. Didn't get it at all. The feel of the thrust of the engines. The noise in your ears. The blur of the ground underneath.

The T-38 was totally different. It was a supersonic jet. Closest thing to a space flight on earth. And he'd loved every single second of it. A few months ago some astronauts had made the fastest journey between earth and the International Space Station, taking just less than six hours. The joke was that it took less time than the standard flight time from London to New York.

He'd love to be a part of something like that. Love it.

The training was over for now and he and Drayton, the other pilot, headed back to the base. As soon as they stepped inside the door they knew something was wrong.

It was as if the temperature had dropped by ten degrees around them.

He shot Drayton a worried look. The silence pervaded the space. Normally this place was full of laughter and chatter.

'Have you heard anything?'

Drayton shook his head. 'No. Not me.'

They dropped their bags and headed through to the main room. All the other candidates were there. Except one.

'What's wrong?' Austin strode into the room and looked from one face to another. No one was talking. No one could look him in the eye. Taryn looked as though she'd been crying. They all looked…broken.

He walked straight up to Adam, their head instructor. 'What is it?'

Adam's gaze flashed between Austin and Drayton. 'It's Lisa. She's sick.'

Austin looked around again. 'What do you mean, she's sick?'

Adam bit his bottom lip. 'She's been diagnosed with non-Hodgkin lymphoma. She starts treatment immediately. She's out of the programme.'

It was as if someone had just kicked him in the guts. He wasn't quite sure if it was the diagnosis, or the outcome. For someone who had their heart set on being an astronaut, it was a double blow.

'Where is she? Can we visit her?'

Adam hesitated. 'She's just been diagnosed. She has to tell her family—tell her kids. Talk to Corrine; she went with her.' He held up his hand. 'But I have to warn you, she's pretty upset too.'

Austin nodded and took off down the corridor. His footsteps slowed as he reached her office. He could hear her. Even from here. The quiet sobs filtered through the door.

He pulled his phone from his pocket. He and Lisa had texted each other regularly. Usually it was picture texts—no words. Just different emoticons. He wanted her to know he was thinking of her. He couldn't send a sad face. That was the wrong message. He certainly couldn't send a crying face. The pictures they normally sent were food, joke animals or—a space shuttle. He certainly couldn't send that.

In the end he picked a heart. A red one had the wrong connotation. So he picked bright blue—the same colour as their WSSA flight suits. Less than ten seconds later she sent it straight back.

He pushed open the door of Corrine's office. It didn't

matter that he hadn't seen her for over a week. It didn't matter that the last time he'd seen her she'd been naked, with only a duvet around her. It didn't matter that he hadn't tried to call her once in the last few days. He could only focus on the right now.

She was sitting on the armchair in the corner of her room, her knees pulled up and her head in her hands.

He knelt down beside her and tugged gently at the edge of her skirt. 'That's a whole different kind of view.'

She looked up. Her eyes were puffy and red. What little make-up she normally wore had all but disappeared. There were a few black smudges around her eyes. As for her hair? It was all over the place.

He didn't wait. He didn't hesitate. He just wrapped his arms around her and pulled her towards him. 'Tell me she's going to be all right. Tell me she will get better.'

It was so odd. A few weeks ago he hadn't known Lisa—hadn't known any of the other astronaut candidates. But things here were so close. The twelve of them were like family to each other—and would be for the next eighteen months. These were the people he'd need to rely on in space. Them, and a whole host of mechanical equipment. You needed to have faith in each other. Needed to trust each other completely.

Yes, there would be other international astronauts on the station—there was a reason they all had to be fluent in Russian—but these were the people who'd been selected at the same time as him. These were the select few that he hoped to have the privilege of going into space with.

He threaded his fingers through Corrine's hair to gently pull her head upwards. 'Tell me,' he whispered.

She shook her head. 'I can't. I just don't know. It's not my speciality. I only know the basics. There are so many different types.'

'But her husband, her kids.'

The tears kept flowing. 'I know. I know. All I can promise is that she's seeing one of the experts. WSSA provides the best medical care in the world. Her care is covered. All types of treatment are covered. Right now, we just have to try and stay positive.'

He smiled weakly. 'And that's why you're just here sobbing your heart out?'

She gave a sigh. 'I just hated it. I hated having to be the one to tell her. To whip her dreams away from right under her nose. It wasn't just the potential diagnosis. It's the whole thing. She'll never be allowed to go into space now, and we both knew that right away.'

She leaned back against the armchair. 'I've only had to do it once before. My job doesn't usually involve the horrible stuff.'

He raised his eyebrows. 'You came to WSSA to get the easy way out?'

'As if. I spend my life telling people if they've failed physicals. If their health isn't up to par to be on the programme. I've even had to break some bad news to astronauts in space. By the time we reach this stage, we've usually screened out just about any possible health condition.'

He pressed his lips together. Things must be really serious for Lisa. He had complete faith in the medical team here, and all the contacts they had. He didn't doubt she would get the best possible treatment available. It didn't make it any easier.

This last week had been a nightmare. The time in the air had been fine—he'd been focused and single-minded about the task in hand. But every time his feet had touched the ground his mind had been filled with her all over again.

Every smile, every frown, every touch of her skin, the feel of her lips on his, the taste of her, the smell of her. When she'd lain next to him and told him this could get addictive he hadn't really understood what that meant.

Twenty-four hours later he had entered withdrawal and he had known *exactly* what she had meant.

He couldn't understand it. Not for one second. Maybe if he saw her a few more times he would get her out of his system for good.

Corrine Carter was messing with his head. And losing a friend and colleague from the programme was messing with his head even more. He couldn't even begin to imagine how devastated Lisa was feeling right now. If he were in her shoes?

It would be his worst nightmare. That one thing you've worked for your whole life to be snatched away.

He stood up and held his hand out to Corrine. 'Come on.'

Her red eyes widened. 'What?'

He didn't care that the other candidates and instructors might be in the corridor. He didn't care that people might see them and comment and ask questions. That didn't seem important right now. 'I'm taking you home.'

She stared at the hand held out before her. He could feel her hesitation, see her waver. 'Come on, Corrine,' he said softly.

She slid her slim hand into his and he closed around it quickly and pulled her up. She tugged her skirt back down and tried to smooth her hair as he led her to the doorway.

He pushed open the door and strode down the corridor. Drayton and Michael were standing in a corner together. Neither of them looked entirely surprised to see Corrine and Austin hand in hand.

Adam acknowledged them with the slightest nod of his head.

There were no questions to be answered. It was clear from the mood that training for today was finished.

Taryn was crying and Lewis, the marine, had his arm wrapped around her. He shook his head as they walked past.

Austin took Corrine out into the streaming Texas sunlight. He walked over to his motorcycle and lifted his spare helmet. He held it out to her and she shook her head.

'What?' He ruffled her hair with his hand. 'It's too late to worry about helmet hair. You've already got it.'

She pointed to the bike and looked down at her skirt. 'I can't get on that.'

He pulled her close. 'Come on, Corrine. Live a little. No one will be able to see anything—just a little bit of leg.' He handed her his leather jacket.

After a few seconds she fastened the helmet and pulled on the leather jacket. He'd already started the engine and was sitting astride the bike, waiting for her.

The first time she tried to swing her leg over, her skirt wasn't high enough. He smirked as she hitched it higher and tried again. This time she swung into the pillion position and fastened her arms tightly around him, snuggling up against his back.

He put the visor on his helmet down and took off. For him the journey was smooth. His motorcycle was his preferred mode of transport, particularly in the Texas heat. His bike hugged the road and Corrine quickly learned to lean with the bike and go with the flow.

The miles between the base and her house were quickly eaten up, but instead of taking the turn towards her winding road he took another turn, leading to a lake he'd passed on the run between her house and the base.

He pulled the bike to a halt and turned the engine off. After a few seconds she swung her leg off the bike and pulled off the helmet. Her hair was sticking up in every direction imaginable.

'I thought you were taking me home.'

'I decided we needed some R & R time.'

She looked at him and then the lake, the corners of her mouth turning upwards. 'You're joking? Right?'

He pulled off his helmet. 'Nope.' He started to unbutton his shirt. 'What do you want to do? Sunbathe? Swim? Or a little game of hide and seek?'

She shook her head and stepped towards him as she shrugged her way out of his leather jacket and let it drop on the grass. 'You know you're crazy.'

He slid his hand through her hair, anchoring his hand at the side of her head. His eyes glanced one way, then another. 'I figure we're all alone. There's no one around. Who owns this lake anyway? Is it you?'

She shook her head. 'It's definitely not me. But I have come here a few times. This place is usually deserted.' She looked up at him. 'I've never been in this lake without a swimsuit.'

He brushed his fingers down the front of her bright blue shirt. 'Well, in that case...' He gave a little tug, freeing her shirt from the waistband of her skirt.

She kicked off her shoes and smiled. There wasn't a single trace of make-up left on her skin. But she'd never looked more beautiful.

She was still looking around. He stepped a little closer. He got that what he was suggesting wasn't normal behaviour for Corrine. He had to know she was all right with this. He put his hand on her hip and put on his best movie voice. 'Lieutenant Commander Mitchell, ma'am.

At your service. I'm an astronaut and I'm going to take you to the stars.'

She threw back her head and laughed. 'This is your line?'

He kept going and waved his hand in the air. 'Let me introduce you to a whole other world.' He nuzzled in at her neck. 'First times can be fun. First time you left a diner with an astronaut and took him home. Now it's time for some skinny dipping.'

She put her hands on his shoulders and murmured in his ear, 'If we get arrested for this I'm letting you take the rap.'

His answer was instant. 'I'm in.'

He threw his shirt onto the grass and tugged his belt from his trousers, glancing up at the sun in the sky. 'It's pretty hot out here. Are you feeling the heat?'

He toyed with the buttons on her shirt, slowly starting to undo the first one. 'Maybe I can help you with this.'

She grinned as she slid her hands around to the back of her skirt, unzipping it and letting it fall onto the grass. His fingers started working quicker. The shirt parted easily, revealing matching bright blue lacy underwear. He blinked. Corrine Carter was full of surprises.

She tilted her head at him and looked towards the lake. 'Fancy a swim, Lieutenant Commander?'

He kicked off his trousers. 'So, we're back to titles, then?'

She nodded as she took a few steps towards the lake. He sucked in a breath at the back view. She glanced over her shoulder. 'I guess so, since I haven't seen you for a week. You have to earn first-name privileges.'

The sun started to warm his shoulders. There was a gentle breeze in the air. The lake was entirely surrounded by trees and greenery. The path he'd driven along was really a footpath. It looked as if their only companions would be the fish.

That suited him just fine.

Corrine stepped calmly out into the lake; his gaze was fixed on the eyeful of backside only covered with a thin strip of blue. She walked until she was waist deep then turned around to face him. 'What's wrong, navy boy?' she teased. 'You scared?'

She leaned back into the water, floating on her back.

He didn't hesitate. He jumped straight in.

The cold knocked the wind from his lungs in shock. It was the last thing he had expected. Texas wasn't just warm. Texas was so hot it must be approaching one hundred degrees. For some reason he'd expected the lake water to be mild—not icy cold.

He emerged from the freezing water, coughing and spluttering after accidentally sucking in some water. As he shook the droplets from his hair all he could hear was the sound of laughter. 'Got you!' shouted Corrine.

He cleared his eyes and took a few strokes towards her. 'You knew it was this cold?'

She nodded. 'It's always this cold.'

He shook his head. 'Why?'

She floated on her back again. 'I have no idea. There must be a scientific reason. I'm just too lazy to find out. I just think of this place as my own ice-cold plunge pool.'

He dived underneath her and grabbed her around the waist, pulling her under next to him. 'Help!' she squealed.

He pushed them both back to the surface and laughed. 'Just wanted to make sure you got the whole experience.'

She shook her hair, splattering him with little droplets as she began to tread water next to him.

She arched her eyebrows at him. 'What's the whole experience, then?'

He laughed and swam closer, his hands skimming her waist again. 'You have such a way with words, Dr Carter. You make them sound so *dirty*.'

She kept a straight face. 'I think we should make a bet.'

He was surprised. 'What's the bet?'

She smiled. 'Loser makes dinner. I might have all the ingredients, but I'm not the best cook. I can give you a personal guarantee that I'll burn anything I attempt to make. So, let's make a bet and the loser makes dinner.'

He'd never had any doubt they'd end up back at her house. It seemed like a given. But this was a direct invitation. And that felt a little different.

But Austin loved a challenge. 'What's the competition?'

Her smile was triumphant. 'What we're doing—treading water.'

He laughed out loud. 'You think you can out tread me?' She must be crazy. She'd watched him in the pool a few weeks ago. She knew how good he was. Ten minutes treading water in his flight suit and tennis shoes had been no problem. He could do this all night.

He started treading water next to her. 'What else we going to do to pass the time?'

She was keeping pace with him, her head and shoulders easily above the water. 'Will I tell you what I've got in my refrigerator and cupboards and you can decide what to make?'

He nodded. 'Okay, cheeky. Impress me.'

'I have chicken.'

There was silence. He turned in the water to face her. Her nose was wrinkled as she stared up at the sky.

'Is that it?'

She was still concentrating. 'I think I might have some green beans—and maybe some salad.'

'You've got to have more than that.'

She shrugged her shoulders in the water, then her eyes lit up. 'I have chocolate.'

'Chocolate and chicken? Sounds like a disaster. What else? You must have some cans in the cupboard.'

She nodded. 'I'm sure I do. Maybe some tomato soup? Some beans.'

He swam right over to her. 'Don't you eat? Who has so little in their cupboards?'

'Rice!' she squealed. 'I've definitely got some rice.' She gave him a wicked glance. 'Getting tired yet? Are your muscles starting to burn?'

'I haven't even heated up yet,' he shot back.

'Want some help?'

'I think, Dr Carter, you're trying to distract me.'

She swam forward with one stroke and wound her arms around his neck. 'Is it working?'

He pulled her under the water with him. 'It might be,' he whispered before the water covered them both.

Two hours later they were lying next to each other in Corrine's bed. No food had been made but they'd made use of her takeaway menus.

She had a warm glow inside. It was foolish. This didn't really mean anything. Austin had only been looking out for her today after how difficult things had been. And she appreciated it. Probably a little bit more than she should.

Austin was currently tracing one of his fingers down her spine. She giggled as the tiny tremors across her skin tickled. 'Feeling better?'

She sighed and nodded. 'I don't want another day like today.'

He pressed his forehead against hers. 'Me either.'

His fingers started to tangle through her hair. 'Zero-gravity training tomorrow.'

She smiled and leaned towards him. 'Oh, yes, the vomit comet.'

He frowned. 'I'm not sure that I like that name.'

She laughed. 'I'm not sure you'll like the clean-up either.'

His hand started skimming its way across her skin again. 'Wanna take bets on who'll vomit first?' His lips started teasing around her ear. 'Or would that be considered unprofessional?'

She nudged a little closer. 'Too late. Me and the other instructors placed our bets already.'

He pulled back. Surprise was written all over his face. 'You're joking?'

She shook her head. 'Of course not. We always do it.'

His gaze narrowed. 'You bet on me to win, didn't you?'

She rolled over in the bed. 'Now, that would be telling. And I don't kiss and tell.'

He tugged at the cover she'd rolled herself in. 'But you'll tell me, won't you?'

'Never,' she teased.

'In that case, I'll just have to make you,' he said as they both rolled off the bed and onto the floor.

# CHAPTER TEN

Since the departure of Lisa it seemed as if the training instructors had upped the ante for the rest of the candidates. The contents of training manuals about the space station and all its functions were drilled into them. Their Russian language tutor worked them hard, conducting some classes and some experiments completely in Russian. Since the Russian Soyuz spacecraft was the only way to the space station it was essential that the astronauts could communicate clearly and effectively with their counterparts.

The vomit-comet trip had been eventful. The plane journey was designed to simulate microgravity by a number of parabolic climbs and descents to give its occupants the sensation of zero gravity. A bit like being on a giant roller coaster. Ultimately it meant that the candidates could experience periods of sustained weightlessness for around twenty-five seconds, interspersed with periods of acceleration as the aircraft pulled out of its dive and readied for the next run. That was why the plane got its name of the vomit comet. Few astronaut trainees came out unscathed. As usual, the clean-up hadn't been fun. One trainee had even spent the next day in bed.

Today, they were somewhere entirely different. Today, they were preparing to be SCUBA qualified. It seemed odd—since they were going into space. But a large part of their training would be spent in the neutral buoyancy laboratory. This huge water tank was used to simulate space walks mimicking weightlessness in space, and had huge full-size mock-ups of the space station, parts of its modules and some of the vehicles used in space.

But, before they could set foot in the neutral buoyancy laboratory, they had to gain their SCUBA qualification—and there were more than one.

The first few sessions had been learned poolside. Today, they were at one of the lakes in Houston, Texas. It was specifically designed for people who loved diving, with numerous dive schools around the edges and a whole host of diving wrecks sunk in the lake for people to explore.

The early-morning sun was rising in the sky as the scuba instructor started giving them instructions.

Austin was restless. He hadn't slept much last night. Too distracted. He'd like to have pretended that his mind had been full of instruction manuals and diagrams. Instead, he'd spent most of the night wondering what on earth he was doing with Corrine Carter.

She was here today, standing at the side with Blair, sipping coffee while the rest of them geared up. She and Blair had been offered the chance to join the diving class but Corrine had declined. It was the most casual he'd seen her dressed while officially at work. She had on a pair of navy Capri pants, flat sandals and a white shirt covered in pale yellow birds. Her blonde hair was tied back and, even though it was early, she had her sunglasses on her head and a WSSA skip hat in her hand.

She was pointing things out around the lake to Blair and showing him on his map what they corresponded to. Austin zipped up his wetsuit and adjusted his mask. Learning the basics of scuba diving wasn't enough. They were going to spend prolonged amounts of time in the neutral buoyancy lab, and while they weren't required to dive to particularly deep levels to work in the lab, they did have to be comfortable underwater for a considerable period of time.

Corrine settled on a bench overlooking the lake. She was here in her capacity of doctor overseeing the astronauts during this particular exercise. If she felt awkward about it she didn't show it at all.

Some of the other candidates had shot a few looks between him and Corrine. But Michael was the only one who'd actually asked what was going on. Austin had blown him off. 'Nothing.' He'd shrugged off the question. 'She was upset the other day. That's all.'

He didn't care that Michael had rolled his eyes and obviously not believed a word of it. He was still trying to get his head around things himself.

Austin Mitchell had never doubted his actions before. And he hated that this time he might be questioning them a little. Was it really such a good idea to have been so brazen about the developing relationship between him and Corrine? At the time he hadn't been thinking clearly. He'd been so worried about Lisa and about how upset Corrine was that he'd prioritised. If there were going to be consequences he'd have to live with them.

Corrine didn't seem worried at all. She was relaxed and laughing around Blair and the candidates as if nothing had happened. Maybe in her head nothing had happened. This was just a casual fling as a result of some chemistry between them both. Chemistry that would ultimately fizzle out. At least that was what he was telling himself.

Each time he took even the slightest glance at her it just reignited every sense in his body. The chemistry on his part hadn't diminished at all. He hated not being sure about things. Relationships had never been a huge focus in his life. They'd come. They'd gone. They had only ever been interludes in his plans to get to space.

He watched as Corrine flung back her head and laughed at something Blair had said, spilling her coffee from her cup. A tiny spike of jealousy flared inside him.

That was a new experience. He'd never really been invested in anyone enough to worry about jealousy. He smiled wryly as he pulled his oxygen tank onto his back. That was probably a pretty lame thought. It made him sound selfish and self-obsessed. He'd always felt focused but maybe others saw it differently.

But what was Corrine to him anyway? He hadn't phoned her since their last encounter. Not because he hadn't wanted to. Just because he didn't want to give her the wrong idea. He hadn't come to WSSA to form a relationship. He'd come to fulfil his life's ambition.

At least that was what he kept telling himself. Corrine was starting to invade most of his thoughts, most of the time. Being around her constantly was definitely distracting.

He liked her nature. He liked the fact she was completely and utterly invested in the astronaut training programme and had worked hard to get there. It made him respect her more; she wanted to work at WSSA too—just not in space.

He liked the business persona she had at work, along with the power suits, and the much more comfortable and sexy way she was at home. It made him smile.

But what he liked best was the way she was quick to answer him back. Corrine Carter gave as good as she got. She wasn't impressed by his Top Gun skills. She wasn't impressed by his career record.

But he knew he'd impressed her when he'd got down on the floor next to her and attempted to help resuscitate

Frank—even though he clearly hadn't been that comfortable. Austin wasn't afraid of a challenge. It didn't matter what the task was—he would always do his absolute best.

But his biggest issue with Corrine was the chemistry. The spark that flared between them. It was off the charts. And that was the thing that had surprised him most. He definitely hadn't expected it.

A little voice in the back of his head—namely his grandmother—kept conjuring up an old story. It concerned how his grandparents had first met; his grandfather had pointed to his grandmother across a street and told his friend he would marry her, and his grandmother had gone home to her mother and said they should start on her wedding dress.

He'd always thought these were made-up fairy stories. That kind of thing didn't happen in real life. Not to anyone he knew. Thunderbolts didn't really exist. It wasn't rational. It was always overrated.

In the last few years every woman he'd dated had introduced him to their friends as 'Austin Mitchell, Top Gun pilot,' usually with a look of supreme smugness on their face. It seemed that being plain Austin Mitchell wasn't enough. That never sat entirely well with him and he usually managed to extricate himself from the relationship within a few weeks.

For the next five to six years he planned to concentrate solely on getting into space. There was no point in forming any long-term attachment when he could be away for three or six months at a time. Lots of guys in the army, navy and air force did. Life in the forces was like that. But that just wasn't Austin's style.

A wife and family had its place in his future plans in a few years' time. But not right now.

The instructor signalled them to enter the lake with some last-minute instructions. Austin took one last look at the map to see what underwater relic he was to explore. Perfect. He'd been given an old wrecked aircraft. He was actually quite interested in seeing what it looked like at the bottom of the lake. The others were spread between an old fire engine, an old boat and part of an old fairground ride to explore. Today should be fine. They weren't going to be bombarded with technical specifications as they were when studying the space station. They weren't going to be drilled on calculations and theories. He just had to do his tasks underwater and let them monitor his health.

He swam beneath the water's surface. It was clear near the surface and murkier as he reached the bottom. The SCUBA gear was fine. The breathing equipment was fine. In a few weeks he'd be in the neutral buoyancy lab dressed in a full spacesuit. It wouldn't be as easy to move then. Apparently the water helped mimic space but nothing could truly replicate the experience—he'd only know that when he finally got there.

The body of the aircraft emerged from the murky depths. It was an old World War II aircraft bomber. His heart gave a little leap. He felt like a schoolkid. He had a picture on his wall of his grandfather standing next to one of these. His aircraft had been nicknamed Ruby Bell and had a picture of a voluptuous redhead in a beautiful red dress painted on the side. He swam around to the side of the plane, trying to make out what was painted on its side. It was difficult to see. The corrosion from being underwater was evident. Most of the plane was so rusty it was a wonder it hadn't just fallen to pieces. He flickered the little torch attached to his wetsuit. It was hard to pick anything out at the bottom of the lake.

There. Something blue. A frill of a dress. He smiled. This aircraft must have been similar to his grandfather's, with a long-forgotten girl painted on the side. He raised up his hand and touched the side of the plane. It was odd doing his little ritual underwater. He closed his eyes for a few seconds. How many guys had flown in this? How many missions? And had it finally been shot down?

It would be interesting to find out. The monitor attached to his shoulder beeped and flashed red. His time was up. He'd met the allotted amount of time underwater and he'd reached the point he was supposed to.

He started to swim upwards to the surface. Something flashed before him. What was that? He slowed his ascent.

There was turmoil in the water above him. That definitely shouldn't be happening. The diving part of the lake was cordoned off from motorboats, jet skis and kayaks. Safety was a priority here.

He waited a few seconds then pushed upwards. The surface was in turmoil. He shook his head to clear his ears. A voice screamed at him from the side of the lake. 'Austin! Austin!'

His eyes skimmed the lakeside. He was at least fifty metres from the water's edge. Corrine was shouting at him. 'Austin, a boy's caught in the water. Can you help?'

On the water around twenty metres away was an abandoned jet bike. It wasn't supposed to be in this part of the water.

He looked around for the rider but no one was in sight. 'I can't see him!' he shouted back to Corrine.

'He was thrown off. I think he landed somewhere over there.' She was pointing at an expanse of water. Austin pushed his mask back over his eyes and put his mouthpiece back in place before diving back under the water.

He hadn't paid much attention to the map of the items sunk under the water. He'd only really looked for the plane he was supposed to reach. It took a few seconds for the structure in front of him to emerge through the dark.

It was the roller coaster. Part of the track was still in place with the roller coaster sitting at the bottom of one of the loops. Austin pulled out his light again and tried to sweep it over the area.

There. He could see something flailing in the water. He swam quickly. A teenage boy was trapped and panicking. Austin felt like panicking too when he saw the state of the boy's arm. It was obviously broken with blood trailing through the water. The boy must have catapulted from the jet bike and hit his arm off the metal frame.

Austin removed his mouthpiece and held it out towards the boy. He was still panicking, still flailing. The last thing he wanted to do was hurt him by grabbing onto him, but it was important he try and get some oxygen into him. He had no idea how long this guy had been underwater.

The boy was tugging at his shorts. That was what was caught—the drawstring around his waist seemed to have entangled in the metal frame.

Austin caught the boy's hand in his. He was in sheer panic mode. His legs were kicking wildly, his wide eyes turned to Austin's. This time Austin was more forceful. This time he pushed the mouthpiece right up to the boy's mouth. Now, he understood. He made a grab for it and sucked in some air.

Austin turned his torch light on the drawstring of the shorts. He couldn't believe they were caught so tightly. It seemed ridiculous but no matter how hard he tugged at them they wouldn't free. What he really needed was a knife to cut the string, but since he was dressed in a wetsuit a knife was the last thing he had.

He started to feel the pressure on his lungs. He needed to breathe. The young boy was still panicking, so Austin shrugged off his oxygen tank and left him with it as he pushed to the surface.

'Have you got him?' Corrine screamed.

He nodded. 'Just taking a breath. He's caught. His shorts are tangled on the roller-coaster framework. I've given him my oxygen tank. Give me a few minutes to free him.' He could see some of the lake first-aiders hurrying towards Corrine carrying a stretcher and some supplies. 'He's broken his arm. It looks nasty.'

Corrine nodded. 'Just get him free. I'll worry about the arm once we get him out.'

Austin took a deep breath and disappeared under the water again.

She watched him disappear with her heart in her mouth. She felt so useless. There was no boat to let her get out there to help. The lake staff had been notified about the accident and were responding quickly. But standing at the side of the lake, waiting for Austin to reappear, was making her antsy.

It wasn't that he wasn't capable. He'd already proved that. But she knew he'd handed his oxygen over to the kid and he was struggling to get him free. Part of her just wanted to dive into the lake to help. But she knew she would be more of a hindrance than a help.

Blair appeared at her side with the portable stretcher. 'Ambulance is on its way. Is he unconscious?'

She shook her head. 'Austin gave him his oxygen tank. He's just trying to get him free.'

'Thank goodness.'

It seemed as though minutes had passed—but they couldn't have, because Austin would have had to come up for air. Or maybe he was sharing the tank with the boy?

Finally his head appeared in the water. He had the teen-age boy in his arms.

Blair moved to the water's edge. 'Over here, Austin.'

Austin swam slowly, still cradling the boy in his arms.

The teenage boy was sobbing, his head against Austin's shoulder, and he made no effort to try and move himself. As soon as she set eyes on his arm she realised why.

The broken bone was clearly visible and the surrounding tissue completely damaged. The bone had erupted through the skin, leaving a wide-open tear. Compound fractures like this were always at a huge risk of infection. And in a lake like this? The very thought made her shudder. He needed out of there and careful treatment as soon as possible.

She gulped and started unpacking sterile dressings from the medical kit. As Austin approached the lake edge the boy flinched at Blair's outstretched arms.

'Don't touch me! Don't touch my arm.'

Austin paused. He was treading water just as she'd seen him do before, but this time he had a whole other person in his arms. The weight must be dragging him down. But he seemed cool and calm.

'How do you want to do this?' he directed towards her.

She leaned forward with Blair, both their arms in the water. 'What's your name?' she called to the boy.

Austin repeated the question in his ear and the boy mumbled a response. 'Mason. His name's Mason.'

'Mason, I'm Corrine Carter. I'm a doctor. We're going to help you and as soon as we get you out of here I'll give you something for that arm. Just hold it steady. I promise. We won't touch it.' She nodded towards Austin. 'Can you boost him up a little?'

Another pair of arms appeared next to her. It was one of the first-aiders. Austin clenched his teeth and tried to boost Mason towards them. No one touched his arm but Mason let out a yelp that echoed around the lake. It was understandable—with an open fracture like that any movement of his body would cause pain in his arm.

They lifted him as best they could out of the lake. Austin didn't hesitate. He pushed up with his forearms, jumping out of the lake and coming to help. Between the four of them they managed to get Mason onto the bright orange portable stretcher.

A motorboat appeared on the lake. The first-aider looked up as his radio beeped. He spoke quickly for a few seconds. 'The ambulance is waiting for us. It's come around the lake as far as it can.' He nodded towards the motorboat. 'Some of the team are just going to retrieve the jet bike and do a check for any more people who shouldn't be on that part of the lake.'

Corrine nodded in sympathy. The team here worked really hard to keep everything as safe as possible. It was a shame when a few reckless teenagers spoiled things for the other lake users.

She opened some sterile saline and poured some onto the sterile dressings. 'Mason, I'm going to lay these gently on your arm while we transport you to the ambulance. Once we get there, I'll give you something for the pain.'

Mason winced and whimpered as she gently laid the wet sterile drapes over his arm. It was important to protect it from any further chance of infection. An open wound and fractured bones could lead to serious, life-threatening infections. She didn't even want to think about what kinds of bacteria were in the lake and already affecting his wound.

There were plenty of hands to help lift the stretcher to the ambulance, where she gave the paramedics a brief rundown on what had happened. It only took a few minutes to connect Mason to the monitoring equipment and get his vitals. The paramedic met her gaze and glanced at Mason's arm. 'Morphine?'

She nodded as he drew the drug up. Mason would really need some strong pain relief before she even touched his arm again.

'How do you want to clean it?'

She lifted the wet gauze and tried to stop from wincing now she had a clear view of the damage. 'How far away are we from the nearest trauma centre?'

Her brain was currently in overdrive. Mason would need a tetanus shot and some IV antibiotics. If they weren't going to be at a trauma centre soon she would have to find some way to administer them.

'It's only about a thirty-minute journey.' She nodded. 'In that case, I'm going to do the absolute basics. There's some debris in the wound that needs to be flushed out.' Mason was whimpering again and she lifted her hand. 'I'm not going to touch or poke or prod it. I promise you. What I am going to do is just pour some more saline over the wound to try and get rid of any dirt and any bugs. We'll leave the rest to the experts at the hospital. Okay?'

The paramedic finished inserting the IV on Mason's other arm and administered the morphine. Corrine waited a few minutes before she lifted the wet swabs away. She held a disposable bowl underneath and gently poured some sterile saline over the fracture site, washing away some of the debris and dirt that was trapped in the wound. Once she was finished she wet some other sterile swabs and covered the site over.

She nodded to the paramedic. 'We'll leave it like that in the meantime.'

She looked at Mason's pale face. 'You're lucky there was someone there to help you today.' She wasn't about to lecture him—the police would probably talk to him at some point—but she wanted him to understand how much danger he'd actually been in.

'Who was the guy?' asked Mason.

'He's called Austin Mitchell. He's one of the astronaut candidates training at WSSA.'

'I was rescued by an astronaut? How cool is that?'

Corrine sighed. It was a typical teenage response. Of course he would think it was cool that an astronaut had rescued him. He wouldn't give any consideration to the fact that coming into a restricted area with a jet bike could actually have injured some of the divers in the water. If Austin, or any of the others, had come up at just the wrong moment…

She couldn't even think about it. These guys had worked so hard for their places on the training programme. Fate had already dealt them one tough card. They didn't need any others.

Austin stuck his head in the back of the ambulance. 'Corrine, are you going with the ambulance?'

She nodded and dug in her pocket for her car keys. 'What's the name of the trauma centre?'

The paramedic looked up. 'It's the Flynn and Grier Memorial Centre.'

She tossed her keys towards Austin. 'Could you get someone to take my car back to the base?'

His gaze was steady. 'Why don't I just follow you to the trauma centre then take you home?'

Her stomach gave a little flip. She wasn't sure exactly where they stood. She hadn't wanted to presume he would do that for her. And there was something about the way he said those words. Although they were very safe and innocuous it almost seemed as if she were getting into trouble.

'Thanks,' she answered brightly, then turned back to her patient.

'That guy's an astronaut?' Mason had that schoolboy-admiration look in his eyes.

'Yes,' said Corrine sharply. 'And you could have taken

his head off, or any one of my other astronaut candidates today. It wasn't your finest move.'

Mason baulked as the paramedic gave her a smile and pulled an oxygen mask over Mason's face. The doors slammed shut behind them and the ambulance started the bumpy journey back to the main road.

Corrine sighed and sat back to monitor her patient. This was going to be a long day.

Austin swallowed as he watched the ambulance disappear up the road ahead of them. Abe Rosen appeared at his side with a bottle of water. 'Here,' he said. 'You did good. One look at that arm nearly had me gagging. Don't know how I'll do when it comes to the first-aid stuff.'

Austin took a welcome slug of the water. Abe was a fellow candidate, but an engineer. He'd been pretty quiet since they'd started training.

Austin looked at him. 'Haven't you got two kids? I thought you would be used to blood and guts and all sorts.'

Abe laughed and shuddered. 'I tend to close my eyes when anything involves body fluids.' He wagged his finger. 'I'll have you know that my claim to fame is that I can change a diaper with my eyes closed.'

'You're really that bad?' He was amazed. He'd just thought all these things went hand in hand with parenthood.

Abe nodded as he walked alongside. 'Oh, yeah. My own personal gag reflex is the smell of regurgitated baby milk. It's even worse when you don't know they've barfed on you and you get a little waft a few hours later and realise it's been on your back the whole time.'

Austin laughed. Abe hadn't said too much before this.

But Austin had his own theory about that. 'So, what do your wife and kids think about you going into space?'

Abe hesitated. 'Let's just say she's anxious that I get back.'

Austin bit his lip. They didn't talk much about the dangers. Even though these were drummed into them at every briefing, every test flight and highlighted in every manual—the fact there might be a tiny possibility that you wouldn't come back didn't really come into the general conversation.

They focused on the positives. How to overcome any problems they might encounter in space. How to plan for any possibility. Even the unlikely Apollo Thirteen scenario, where you had to think about every tiny piece of equipment available on the space or command module and how it could be used to get you back home.

'What about the kids?'

Abe shrugged. 'They think it's great. Daddy is going into space. Brody just asked me if I'd meet his favourite cartoon character. It's not real to them. Daddy always worked in a lab before. This is much more exciting.'

'You couldn't have done all this before you got married and had kids?'

Abe gave him a thoughtful glance. It was almost as if he could see exactly where Austin's train of thought was going.

He nodded. 'Maybe—in an ideal world. But...' he held his hands up towards space '...before I met Anne...once I got into space I would have wanted to stay there. The space station wouldn't have been enough. I would have been the guy who was signing up for the one-way mission to Mars. Now, I have something to come home to. Anne and the kids ground me. They make me realise that what I do is just a tiny part of things.'

He nudged Austin. 'Believe it or not, the world doesn't revolve around you and me. It'll keep on turning whether we're here or not.'

Austin nodded. His mind was swimming. He didn't even want to acknowledge the kind of things that were floating around in there. Because those kinds of thoughts weren't *him*. They never had been.

'Maybe you need someone to ground you too.'

It was like a whole snow dump over his head. It didn't matter that he might be a little cold anyway, walking along the side of the lake in his wetsuit. A shiver worked its way down his spine. His whole head was playing games with him.

Right now, if he closed his eyes for a second he could see Corrine, sitting in her shorts, on her rocker on the porch of that yellow clapboard house. That was what made him feel grounded right now. And he didn't like it. Not one bit.

Trouble was, he was starting to get a little of what Abe said. The world didn't revolve around him. And when you'd spent most of your life as a selfish so-and-so it was a bit of an adjustment.

His friends probably wouldn't call him selfish. He'd do anyone a good turn. They would probably call him single-minded.

But it wasn't just Corrine on his brain. He'd had another call from the Head of Research at the university. They still wanted him. But the reality was they couldn't wait for him. The research needed to be started in the next year. He would still be completing his astronaut training. Then, if he was successful, he'd have to wait his turn to be scheduled for a mission. Chances were he'd spend the next ten years of his life here at WSSA—just as he'd planned.

The timing drove him crazy. The cancer research

needed to be done now. Not in ten years' time. He got that. He really did.

But the Corrine stuff? It was driving him even more crazy.

It wasn't just the insane chemistry and attraction. It wasn't just the sex. It was all the distracting stuff around about that.

He'd never met a woman who'd captured his attention like Corrine. He'd never actually been with a woman that he wanted to spend every single day with. A few dates a week had been fine. Sometimes even too much. But Corrine was different. Work kept that apart. And for the first time in his life he actually resented that a little.

Something had changed in him. Something had altered. It was as if the earth's gravitational pull had just tilted a little. And it had put him on a collision course with her.

He'd had women declare that they loved him before. He'd had women weep and wail when he'd finished with them. But everything about Corrine was different.

She kept him guessing. He didn't even know if she really liked him.

He'd had to control the spurt of rage that he'd felt when she'd revealed an ex had hurt her in the past. If he ever found out who that was…he didn't want to be responsible for his actions.

And he wouldn't even care that those actions would probably get him thrown off this programme.

*That was it.* That was what was scaring him so much. The strength of his emotions for Corrine. It was making him think thoughts like that.

Then there was the fact that Corrine had just treated him as if he were some casual passer-by.

There. That was what stung the most today. It was almost as if she hadn't even considered the fact he might drive her car and pick her up. He couldn't work out if she was just distracted by doing her job, or she was trying to keep a professional distance between them. Or if she really didn't care at all.

It surprised him how much that burned.

Abe touched his arm and nodded in the direction of the ambulance. 'Guess you'd better go and get our doc.'

Austin tried to keep his voice level. 'I guess I'd better.'

# CHAPTER ELEVEN

'YOU'VE BEEN TRANSFERRED over to me.'

'What? Why?' Austin couldn't quite believe what he was hearing. Blair King was sitting behind the desk, tapping away on his computer. The printer beside him whirred and Blair pulled out a multi-coloured chart.

'Here's your training programme.'

Just what he needed. Another training programme. He glanced down at it. 'Why have I been transferred over to you?'

Blair didn't meet his eyes. 'Dr Carter thought it would be for the best.'

'Really?'

His instant reaction was anger. She'd dumped him? She hadn't mentioned this when they'd been in bed together last night.

Then the rational part of his brain started to kick in. She'd transferred him. That didn't mean she'd dumped him. It meant that she didn't want either of them to get into trouble regarding their relationship.

Just about everyone knew they were seeing each other by now.

And he got that. He understood. But he didn't understand why she hadn't discussed it with him first. How long would it have taken? Ten seconds. A roll over in bed. Oh, by the way, Austin, I don't want to get accused of special treatment. You getting it, and me giving it. I've transferred your care to another doctor. Easy.

Blair was still staring at him. There was an amused expression on his face. It was almost as if he was waiting to see how Austin would react.

He gritted his teeth. 'It will be a pleasure working with you, Doc,' he muttered before turning on his heel and walking out.

His phone rang almost instantly. He pulled it from his flight suit. 'Yeah?'

He hadn't even looked at the screen. 'Austin?'

Darn it. It was his father. The most astute man on the planet. 'Oh, sorry, hi, Dad.'

'What's wrong?'

'Nothing.' He started striding down the corridor, glancing in rooms as he passed, looking for her blonde hair.

'Tell that to someone who believes it.'

His footsteps halted. It had been more than thirty years but he'd never been able to pull the wool over his father's eyes.

'Is it problems with the astronaut training?' He could hear the tension in his father's voice. The last thing he wanted to do was upset him.

'Of course not. There're no problems at all.'

'You're still going to Kazakhstan tomorrow?'

He let out a sigh. 'Yes. I'm still going.' It was the next part of the training. They had to learn to pilot the shuttles with the Russian crew as that was currently the only mode of transport to the space station. The training was intense. He would spend the next four weeks speaking only Russian and learning to fly a new spacecraft. It wasn't for the faint-hearted.

Or those who were having mixed feelings.

'Well, that's fine, then. With your piloting skills I expect you to ace everything.'

No pressure, then. Austin drew in a breath. The family traditions had always been there, hanging over his head like a goal he had to meet. Up until this point it had pretty much been his dream too—he'd never really thought about anything else. He'd never even had a discussion with his father about any other possibilities. He spoke before he changed his mind.

'I've been offered another job. A real opportunity.'

There was silence at the end of the phone. He couldn't really blame his dad. This must be a real bolt from the blue.

'Oh.'

He kept talking. It was easier to fill the silence. 'It's research into cancer. All about cell growth in certain cancers and whether we can actually switch those cells off.'

His father's voice was steady. 'But why would you want to be stuck in a lab? You're just about to head off into space. It's been your dream since you were a boy. We still have the stars stuck to the ceiling in your bedroom.'

Austin felt his stomach plummet. Of course they did. His parents had always encouraged his ambitions and he'd never let them know that he might have others. They'd been so taken by him carrying on the family tradition of flying, then trying for the space programme, that there had hardly been room to acknowledge or talk about his microbiology research. He'd always been so focused. So sure about what he wanted to do.

Or was he?

He was trying not to acknowledge the fact that a tiny fire had been lit inside him when he'd been asked to head the cancer research team. It was an honour. A privilege. Not that anyone would blame him if he chose to be an astronaut instead—well, no one except his family. Potentially cure cancer or go to space: they were two totally different but completely fantastic opportunities.

But then there was something else—something much more overwhelming. Corrine. The feelings he was having…the doubts. If Corrine ever met his parents he wanted them to love her, embrace her into the family. If his father thought for a second that he'd given up his dream of being an astronaut for a woman…

No. He just couldn't go there. He wouldn't let her be the focus of any bitterness. Much better to plant the seed in his father's mind about another job.

He didn't need to know the real reason Austin was having second thoughts.

He kept his voice low. 'Imagine the difference to the world, Dad, if I found a way to switch off the cancer cells. Imagine the lives that could be saved.'

There were a few more seconds of silence. He'd never laid this out on the line before. He wasn't even thinking about himself. Chances were, research like this could mean a Nobel Prize. But he was thinking about all the other people—people like Frank the instructor's wife, whose life had been cut short. Maybe the stress of losing his wife had contributed to Frank's heart attack?

His dad cleared his throat. 'So, Kazakhstan. When do you leave?'

The subject was closed for now. And a tiny part of him was disappointed. It didn't matter that his brain didn't know which way was up. Right now, he felt as if he were back on the vomit comet.

He started walking back down the corridor, talking to his dad about the travel arrangements. By the time he was finished he'd reached the entrance way and there had been no sign of Corrine.

Maybe this was the way she wanted to play it. Keeping her distance from him.

He had no idea what was going on here. As soon as they were in each other's company things just seemed to spark. It felt as if she were a magnet that pulled him towards her. She certainly hadn't given any sign that his attentions were unwelcome. So what was going on?

He pushed open the door and headed towards his bike. And stopped.

She was leaning against it. And he felt a jolt. His eyes took in her tousled hair, black leather jacket, white shirt and business skirt. Her stiletto heels were firmly in place and her legs were crossed as she leaned back against the bike with her arms folded across her chest.

She didn't move as he approached her.

He tried not to smile. He tried to admit the fact he was actually happy to see her.

Other parts of him were currently in a spin cycle. This woman was messing with his brain and his focus.

The sun was streaming behind her, lighting up her oh-so-curvy silhouette. She had sunglasses in place, hiding the expression in her green eyes.

He stopped a foot away, letting the breeze carry her orange scent towards him. 'It seems I've been dumped.'

She tilted her chin towards him. 'You haven't been dumped. You've just been reassigned.'

'Don't I get a say in that?'

'No.' He was struck by the curtness of her words.

He stepped forward. 'So what do I get a say in?'

She uncrossed her arms and put her hands on his hips, tilting her chin up towards him. 'You get a say in whether you give me a lift home or not.' Her words were sultry, almost whispered, and she ran one finger up the front of his chest.

He caught it in his hand.

She moved closer, pressing her body against his. 'Four weeks is a long time. And Kazakhstan is a long way away.'

There was a smile playing around the edges of her lips. She knew exactly what she was doing to him.

'You think you can get on my bike in that skirt?'

She grinned. 'Oh, I know I can,' and in the blink of an eye she hiked up her skirt and swung her leg over the bike. Now it was barely covering the parts it should.

He almost growled, looking around to see if anyone was watching and grabbing the helmets for the bike. Within a few seconds he was on board and the engine was fired up. 'Hold on,' he shouted as he let the throttle go. 'You're in for the ride of your life!'

Everything about this was odd. She loved the feeling of being in control. She loved the fact that even though Austin was all man, she didn't have a single doubt about the fact he let her make the rules.

He'd picked up on her vibes, her need for control. The fact that he wasn't afraid to let her be in charge only increased his sex appeal in her eyes.

She glanced at the clock. It was only an hour until his pick-up. He was lying fast asleep in her bed. She ran a finger down his arm. 'Hey, Bates. It's your wake-up call. Kazakhstan is calling.'

He flinched and she frowned. Maybe he was just sleepy.

His eyes flickered open. He licked his lips and his dark eyes focused on hers. 'What're your plans for the next few weeks?'

She shrugged. 'Some of the candidates will still be here. I'll be heading down to Key Largo with the rest of the team for more training.'

He rolled over onto his back. 'So, I'll be freezing in Kazakhstan and you'll be wearing your bikini in Key Largo?'

She smiled. 'Pretty much.' She slid her hand across his stomach. 'What's the problem? It's all part of the training. It's the only way you'll get up into space.'

His eyes twinkled. 'Well, that, and sleeping with the WSSA doctor. Can I get a prescription for this?'

She picked up her pillow and thumped him with it. It didn't take long for him to join in the pillow fight and before she knew it her bedroom was littered with floating feathers that fluttered around them like wedding confetti.

She held out her hands and laughed as they started drifting to the ground. Austin picked up his phone and snapped a photo.

'What? What are you doing?'

'I need something to look at for the next four weeks.' He spun the phone around. 'This will do nicely.'

It was like a sugar rush going through her body. The weirdest of sensations. She felt happy. She felt relaxed. It didn't matter that her hair was completely mussed up. It didn't matter that she was dressed only in her underwear. She felt completely happy in her own skin as the feathers floated around her.

And the glow. The weirdest glow... She'd never had that before.

She thumped back down onto the bed. 'Show anyone else that picture and I'll do you a serious injury.'

Four weeks without Austin. She kind of wanted to ask for a picture of him in return.

This was the problem with not having had many serious relationships. This was the problem with spending the last few years being relatively selfish and only concentrating on herself and her career.

This was the first time in a long time that anyone that

felt even mildly like the 'right' guy had come along. Trouble was, she didn't know what to do with him.

She didn't know what came next.

Should she say something? Do something?

Austin glanced at the clock, then swung his leg over her body, putting his hands at either side of her head.

'Fifty minutes. Fifty minutes until pick up.' He started kissing around her neck. 'Any idea what we could do to kill some time?'

She blinked and kept her face straight. But darn…he was distracting her again. Those kisses were setting off little rocket ships throughout her body. She ran her fingers down his spine. 'We could talk about space modules.'

He lifted his head from her neck and pressed his full body weight against her. There was very little material between them.

*I'll miss you.* Those were the words she wanted to say. Those were the words that were imprinted on her brain. But even those three little words would take her another step. Another step away from being totally in control. To leaving herself emotionally vulnerable.

This guy was already peeling back her layers. He made her laugh. He made her heartbeat quicken at the sound of his voice. He made her comfortable.

She'd never have let any of her ex-boyfriends have a picture of her in her underwear. She'd never have trusted them enough.

But with Austin it just seemed…right.

And her head was struggling with that.

He stopped kissing her neck and poised above her again. Those electric-blue eyes were mesmerising. 'Promise me one thing.'

Her stomach clenched. This sounded serious. They usually kept things pretty light-hearted. Was he wrestling with the same emotions as she was?

The hottest astronaut candidate in the world, virtually naked in her bed...as if she were going to say no!

'What?'

He started kissing down her body. 'Promise me, that in four weeks, when I come back from Kazakhstan, I'll find you in the exact same position as I'm going to leave you.'

She pulled him back up towards her and wrapped her arms around his neck. 'Well, that depends.'

'Depends on what?'

'On what my farewell gift is.'

He grinned. 'Let me show you.'

And he did.

# CHAPTER TWELVE

HE'D ACED EVERYTHING. Every language test. Every piloting test.

Four weeks of complete and utter focus.

There wasn't much to do here in Kazakhstan. Sure, they had access to computers and the Internet. But the space training centre was out in the back of beyond. There was no chance of visiting a bar and allowing yourself to slip into oblivion for a few hours. Every spare second, by every candidate, was spent studying. If anyone failed here, it was goodbye and go home. And everyone was far too invested to let that happen.

Everyone but him.

He was still ignoring things. Still giving the impression that space was all he'd ever dreamed of. He wasn't quite sure when that dream had shifted. But it seemed to be right around the time he'd met Corrine. And that bugged him.

Bugged him that he couldn't work out if it was how he felt about her that was affecting things, or if, by some weird coincidence, he'd let the stuff that had always been there finally come to the surface.

He was becoming someone he didn't recognise. For the first two weeks they'd exchanged cheeky emails thick and fast. He'd kept bugging her for a picture of her in a bikini at Key Largo. Finally she'd sent one.

It was a selfie. The best selfie he'd ever seen. She was sitting on the edge of a boat, the beautiful blue ocean behind her, wind in her hair and dressed only in a leopard-print bikini. If spontaneous combustion were possible he was right there.

Then, the Internet had crashed.

Most of the candidates thought it was deliberate to make them focus on their tasks.

But Austin had found himself focusing on the photo on his phone.

He actually couldn't believe how much he missed her. He wanted to know who'd been on the boat with her. And he recognised the little twinge of jealousy in his stomach. It was the second time he'd felt one about Corrine. No other woman had ever sparked the same emotions.

It felt...unnatural. At least for him.

He'd never felt this way about a woman before. And it was driving him plain crazy.

Four weeks. That was all this was. Four lousy weeks.

How on earth would he survive three or six months on the space station?

He needed to sort himself out. He needed to know what he actually wanted before he could make any next move.

Maybe if he told her he was giving up the astronaut training she wouldn't be interested any more. Maybe she was only keen on a guy who had the same interests as her. A research professor might bore her completely. A hotshot pilot and astronaut would have way more sex appeal than a lab guy.

And what about his family? What about his parents and grandparents? How could he disappoint them after all this time? Would they resent Corrine? Would they think that she'd changed his mind? Would his colleagues think he'd met a woman and decided space wasn't the dream destination after all? He'd never hear the end of it.

He shook his head. He'd thought being here would make him more focused. Instead, he felt more confused by the second.

But there was one thought that was central in his mind. Corrine Carter. He missed her.

He hadn't figured on that.

And he'd really missed her. He'd missed her smile. He'd missed her green eyes with little brown flecks. He'd missed her curves and the way she wore her suits so well. He'd missed her matching underwear. He'd missed the smell of her, the touch of her, the taste of her.

Every time he closed his eyes he saw her. Corrine, in her bright blue underwear with her blonde hair mussed up around her face. She was laughing. She was happy. She was sexy as…

Enough. It had to be enough.

If he wanted to stay focused on space he had to stay away from Corrine.

There was nothing else for it. She was like a drug to him. An addictive drug.

And he hated being that weak. He hated the fact that he was thinking about her when he should be focusing on piloting the shuttle.

He couldn't do that. He couldn't afford to do that in space. Not having his mind on the job could cost him his life, as well as the lives of the rest of the crew.

He couldn't take that risk. Not for a heartbeat.

Tomorrow was home time. Tomorrow he'd be back in Texas.

Tomorrow he had to break up with Corrine.

It was—quite possibly—the longest two minutes in her life.

It had taken a few weeks to realise that the permanent

knot feeling in her stomach and lack of appetite might actually be something else and not just a dodgy tummy she'd picked up in Key Largo.

And after two weeks of lots of flirty emails, she'd had not a word from Kazakhstan. Not a single blooming word.

She was already feeling terrible. Hearing nothing just made her feel ten times worse.

She glanced at her watch. Another minute to wait. She stood up and quickly realised she didn't need to wait. One word. Pregnant.

No chance for misunderstanding. The digital display was quite clear.

Her legs wobbled and she slid down the wall, putting her head in her hands and sucking in a few deep breaths.

This was so *not* in her life plan. Single motherhood. Perfect. Just perfect.

How could she work full time at WSSA and look after a baby? She didn't even have family nearby to help. They were thousands of miles away and a few states over.

And it wouldn't exactly take her colleagues long to work out whose baby it was. With her luck little Jimmy would appear in a flight suit with a pilot's licence in his hand, sucking people in with his father's signature bright blue eyes.

She gulped and stood up. It was time to get a grip. She rested her hand on her perfectly flat stomach. She was barely pregnant. No one would have to know for a while. She had plenty of time to make plans.

She let her head fall back against the cool tiles. She'd need to see an OB/GYN. And she certainly wouldn't see one around here. She'd like her business to stay her business for the next few weeks. The gossiping could wait.

Her stomach lurched. Austin. How would she tell Austin?

Because of course she'd need to tell him. It wasn't as if she could keep this secret for long.

Just the thought of it was like a weight pressing down on her chest. They'd never, ever discussed anything like this. Kids hadn't been on his radar—just as they hadn't been on hers. For now, anyway.

Of course in the future she'd imagined herself having a family once she'd finally found the perfect man. It just seemed she was doing everything in the wrong order.

Trouble was, in a way, she'd found the perfect man. Austin was perfect in so many ways. He might even be happy about this.

But they weren't ready for this. *She* wasn't ready for this.

She'd just started to let him in. For the first time ever, she'd started to let her emotions affect her. She'd let herself be ruled by her heart instead of her head.

She didn't want this relationship to be forced. Did they even officially have a relationship? She'd wanted to let things evolve naturally—to see where they ended up.

But she had the sneaking suspicion Mr Hotshot was probably a bit traditional, and as soon as she told him he might want to 'do the right thing'.

And the truth was she didn't want to be his 'right thing'; she wanted to be the love of his life.

Wow. Where had that come from?

How did you go from flirting with a guy, to sleeping with a guy, to making him the love of your life? The thought terrified her.

What would a life with Austin be like? She'd never done this before. Never even imagined having a life with someone else. How would they cope with a baby? Would he want to stay here, or somewhere else? How would she

feel when he shot off into space for six months and left
her at home?

It was all too overwhelming. Too much to consider
when she'd just discovered her life was already going to
change completely.

She absolutely couldn't go there right now. She just
couldn't. There was other stuff to deal with. Emotions
would have to wait.

She took a long slow breath and blew out slowly. Positive thoughts. Positive thoughts. That was what she needed
to think.

She didn't want her kid to feel unwanted. He or she
might have been unplanned, but her son or daughter definitely wouldn't be unwanted. Life was going to have to
change and she'd just have to learn to adapt.

As for Austin? She'd no clue where he would fit into
this picture.

Even if she secretly hoped it would be right by her side.

# CHAPTER THIRTEEN

HE HADN'T APPEARED. The astronaut candidates had arrived home last night and Austin hadn't appeared at her house.

What was worse was she'd actually waited. She'd waited for him in her bed.

It had seemed exciting at the time. She'd had it all planned out in her head. He'd arrive, find her waiting exactly as he'd left her before, they'd kiss, she'd tell him the news and…

Forget it. None of it had happened. After lying in her underwear for two hours she'd finally got up and eaten some chocolate, cursing him that she couldn't drink wine.

The excuses had flown around her head. He was sick. He'd been called away for a family emergency. He'd had to help a friend with something.

She was trying really hard to cling onto something positive. Although she hated how desperate that made her feel. She had to reserve judgement until she'd actually spoken to him and that would be some time today.

She pulled up the training sheet. Today was D-day for some of the candidates. At this point, any candidate who wasn't making the grade would be transferred out of the programme.

Austin's name was in the top spot on nearly every sheet.

He'd aced just about everything. He was a dead cert for astronaut selection.

She didn't know whether to be happy or sad.

It was just what he wanted. His mission to the space station would probably last around six months. Six months for him to be absent from his baby's life.

She squeezed her eyes closed for a second. She had to stop thinking like this. Lots of astronauts had families. They had to leave behind husbands, wives, partners and children to go and fulfil their dream. There was nothing wrong with that. Nothing. She'd always believed that. So, why now did it seem so much harder?

Why did six months seem like a lifetime?

She gave herself a shake and walked over to the coffee pot in her room. Two seconds later she turned and walked away. Old habits were hard to break. She'd need to find some decaf somewhere.

There was too much going on in her head right now. The whole pregnancy thing was overwhelming. Which was pathetic really, since she was a professional with a good job and her own place. She didn't need anyone else. She could do this on her own.

It didn't matter that this wasn't how she had imagined things would work out. At no point in any of the half-erotic dreams she'd been having had her abdomen been swollen with a baby. The main feature of any of these dreams had been Austin. He'd been front and centre in them all. But where would he figure in her life now?

She bit her lip and walked out of her office, stalking down the corridor to Frank's room. He might not be at work but she was sure he'd have decaf somewhere. Three minutes later she had the prize, along with an unopened packet of chocolate-chip cookies. Bonus.

She walked back to her office and straight into the large immovable force currently blocking her door.

'Oof!'

The broad shoulders turned round immediately. Austin. Bright blue eyes. Staring straight at her.

'Sorry. We need to talk.'

*Boy, do we.*

She started to put some decaf into the coffee pot and tried to stop her hands from shaking. 'Yes, I think we do. I have some news.'

Austin folded his arms and leaned against the door jamb. Why did he have to look so darn sexy?

But the hardest thing was the fact she just wanted to go over and touch him. Smell him. Stand next to him. That was why keeping her hands busy was the best thing for her.

'Corrine...' His voice tailed off.

It was the *way* he said her name. As if he were born to say her name. She loved it. She loved the Texas drawl that sent so many shivers up her spine. But there was something about the way his sentence started but didn't continue that made her turn around.

'Aren't you supposed to be at the selection meeting?'

He pressed his lips together. 'This is more important.'

*You're right, it is.*

Had he really just said that? She was stunned. The guy who had one focus, one ambition in life—to be astronaut. *This* was more important?

It threw her. She wasn't expecting that. She'd been so busy trying to think of when she should tell him about the pregnancy that it hadn't occurred to her he would be thinking of anything but the selection meeting this morning.

She couldn't react to his words. Was there a possibility that he already knew? How could that even be possible? But one thing was clear. She wasn't going to stand in the way of his dream. Not her. And not her baby. She couldn't be that person.

But there was something else. Something emanating from him.

And it didn't feel good. The vibes just didn't feel right.

She had to stop her hand from automatically going to her stomach. Protective. That was how she felt already about the baby growing inside her.

He hadn't moved over next to her. He hadn't tried to touch her. And he wasn't smiling. She could almost see the imaginary silver helium balloon with *I'm pregnant* on it floating off into the sky.

He started again. 'Corrine, being away gave me some time to think.'

'Think about what?'

'Think about us.'

Okay. How come a little part of her just died inside?

He could barely look at her. Oh, he was looking at her, but those blue eyes weren't fixed on her as they normally were. He couldn't hold her gaze for more than a few seconds.

'What is it you want to say, Austin?'

Her head was screaming at her. *Don't ask that question—you won't like the answer.*

A few figures dressed in bright blue flight suits passed the open doorway. The rest of the candidates were on their way to the selection meeting.

Austin took a deep breath. 'Corrine, you know I like you.'

Like. The word every woman wanted to hear.

She didn't respond. She couldn't respond.

'You know I respect you...'

Here it came. The 'Dear John' speech.

'But this astronaut selection, the training, it's too important to me right now. I've worked my whole life for this. I can't afford any distractions. I need to keep my head entirely focused on the job.'

She could feel tears pooling in her eyes and a little surge of anger flickered through her. All those ridiculous fanciful dreams she might have had about a happy ever after. How stupid had she been?

'It's fine, Austin.' It was all she could manage.

But Austin wasn't finished. 'Actually, Corrine, it's not fine.' He glanced over his shoulder to make sure no one was listening. 'I've been having doubts.'

'What?' Her head shot up. It was the last thing she'd expected to hear.

'I've been having doubts about the programme.'

'Why?' Of all the things he could have said this was the one that surprised her most.

His gaze fixed on her. 'I've been having doubts because of you.'

It was as if he had taken her lungs with both hands and just squeezed all the air out of them.

'What?' It came out kind of strangled.

It felt like the worst thing he could say to her. *She* was the reason he was doubting the dream he'd always had of being an astronaut?

He was staring at the floor right now. 'Kazakhstan gave me some time to think. I might have aced the tests but my mind wasn't always on the job.'

He knew. He knew he'd aced the tests. He probably knew what would happen next.

He shook his head. 'I can't do that. I can't be *that* guy. That guy who is thinking about a girl back home when he should be focusing on the job. I have the lives of other astronauts to think about.' He pointed upwards. 'Every man and woman up there has trained their whole life to get there. They need a pilot who is one hundred per cent focused. That's the way I always was before. And that's the way I need to be again. I'm sorry.'

She was going to be sick. She was going to be sick, right now, all over this carpet.

Other women might love this. Love the fact that they'd affected a guy so much he couldn't concentrate at work.

She knew better. She knew exactly the risks involved in having a pilot who wasn't focused on the job. She understood them better than anyone.

She'd done this to him. She'd let their flirtation build into something else entirely. She'd let her emotions get involved. She'd let her guard down.

She squeezed her eyes closed for a second. She couldn't tell him about the baby. She just couldn't. Right now, for Austin, it would be the worst news possible.

If he couldn't focus because of her, it would only be worse if she told him about the baby.

That was the one thing that was crystal clear right now.

She felt her doctor mask slip into place. The one she used when she was about to tell someone bad news. She could do this. She could.

She took a deep breath and met his gaze. 'I understand what you're saying, Austin. And you're right. You have to keep your mind totally on the job. That's best for everyone. Let's just leave it at that.'

Her heart was breaking. It was breaking in two right now.

She lifted the coffee pot to pour from it, praying he wouldn't see her shaking hand. 'I think you have somewhere else to be. You'd best not be late.'

He blinked. He looked a little surprised. What had he expected? For her to weep and wail and ask him not to dump her?

'Good luck,' she added with a pasted-on smile.

He gave her a nod and walked out of the room, and out of her life.

His head was spinning and he couldn't think straight. Corrine had the best poker face in the world. Was she upset? Was she angry?

He just didn't know. He felt like the worst person on the planet. Lower than the belly of a snake. Every single part of him wanted to march back into that room and say he'd made a mistake. Every single cell in his body was screaming at him. He should have told her that he loved her—not that he was walking away.

He stopped for a second and ran his fingers through his hair. Maybe he was wrong about all this. Maybe this wasn't a big deal to her. Maybe the reason she'd seemed so cool was that she didn't really care. He was just another guy.

His gut twisted. He would probably hate that more than anything.

Michael walked up behind him and slapped him on the back. 'Come on, big guy, let's find out if they're sending us to the stars.'

Of course. Focus. That was what he should be doing. If he hadn't met Corrine he'd probably have spent all night worrying about today's selection. Instead, he'd spent all night figuring out how to break up with her.

It was time to get his mind back on the job. He walked into the room behind Michael.

Adam, the former astronaut and main instructor, stood in front of the class with a clipboard in his hand. It didn't matter that he was surrounded by technology. He still liked to do things his way.

He surveyed the room. 'You'll know that the selection today is based on all the training and testing you've done over the last three months. At this stage, we're going to tell you who will be on the first astronaut selection team.' He looked around the class. 'You all understand that health issues can dictate that someone is excluded from the programme. But based on our recent testing our first team will be—'

You could hear the sharp intake of breath all around him. His heart should be beating against his chest. He should be breaking into a sweat right now, his stomach clenched, waiting to see if his name would be called. So, why wasn't he?

He'd just given up the woman he loved for this.

Space had better be worth it because his pride was still alive and fighting.

Adam shot him a smile. 'Our pilot will be Austin Mitchell. Our crew, Taryn Peters, Michael Fisk and Lewis Donnell.'

Michael and Lewis jumped from their seats, whooping and laughing. Taryn was quick to join them. A few other candidates turned to stare at him. They must be wondering why he wasn't doing the same.

He pasted a smile onto his face and stood up, shaking hands with those nearest to him. First crew. This was a huge deal. This was the thing he'd spent the last few years dreaming of. He should be elated. And he just couldn't understand why he wasn't.

After the initial jubilations they sat back down. A second crew was called and a few candidates transferred to other spots within WSSA. Astronaut training wasn't for everyone. No matter how much they prepared beforehand.

When they finally finished, Michael slung his arm around Austin's shoulders. 'Celebratory drink?'

Austin nodded. 'Sure. Just let me call my dad.'

It felt bittersweet. Part of him was living his dad's dream and part of him was stealing it.

This should be the happiest day of his life.

So why wasn't it?

# CHAPTER FOURTEEN

SHE WAS SITTING on her porch eating what looked like fried chicken, coleslaw and salad. She frowned as he pulled up right at her steps.

She'd changed out of her suit into her barely there shorts and a simple T-shirt. She looked much more relaxed like this. He liked her this way.

He looked out across the fields. From here, it felt as if this house were in the middle of nowhere. A little sanctuary just outside the city where time could be suspended for a little while.

'What do you want, Austin?' she said as he climbed off the bike.

'I wanted to clear the air between us. I don't want there to be an atmosphere at work.'

She glared at him. 'I'm a professional at work. Just the way I should be. You've nothing to worry about.' She stood up and picked up her plate. 'Go home, the conversation is over.'

He flinched. What had he expected?

She'd headed towards her front door but then turned around and narrowed her gaze, walking back over to the railing. Memories swamped him. This was where he'd first kissed her. Just like now, him on one side of the railing, her on the other.

'Actually, I've just realised I'm not at work. So I don't need to be professional.' She had a fiery glint in her eye. Sass. This was why he liked her so much.

She held out her hand. 'Give me your phone.'

'What?'

'Give me your phone. You've got pictures of me on it that I want to delete.'

He dug into the back pocket of his jeans and pulled out his phone. The last thing he wanted her to do was to delete her pictures.

She leaned over the railing and grabbed it just as it beeped. She pressed a few buttons then handed it back, her lips pressed tightly together. She was gorgeous when she was angry.

'Congratulations on making the crew. Enjoy yourself in the stars, Lieutenant Commander Mitchell.'

He glanced at the phone. A message from his father. He pushed it back in his pocket.

Corrine had moved again, her hip bumping her front door open. She was leaving. She was finished with him.

'It doesn't feel like it should.' The words came out before he could stop them.

She hesitated. 'What?'

It was too late to pull them back. He ran his fingers through his hair and fixed his view on the horizon. 'Being picked. It doesn't feel like I thought it would.'

He could see her wavering—trying to decide whether to go inside or whether to keep talking to him. She sighed and turned a little more towards him. 'What did you think it would feel like?'

'Fantastic. Brilliant. Amazing. I thought I would be over the moon.'

Her clear green eyes fixed on his. She looked puzzled. 'And you're not?'

'No. I'm not.' He winced. Saying those words out loud just seemed so wrong. Almost as if they were talking about someone else. Someone who hadn't chased this dream their entire life.

Corrine sucked in a breath. It was clear she was shocked. 'What's this all about?' She moved uncomfortably on the step next to him. 'I don't get it. From the moment I've met you everything has been about this. This moment. This time.' She lifted her hands. 'Getting up into the stars.'

He looked upwards too. It was still daytime. The sky was bright blue. Maybe if it had been night and the sky were lit up with stars it would have made things clearer.

He would be able to tell if he felt that familiar tug when he searched the night sky and wondered when he would be up there.

He ran his fingers through his hair. He'd never had doubts before. His life's course had been set. Sure, there was some pressure from his family about being a pilot— family 'heritage' and all that. But he'd loved the freedom of flying through the skies. He'd never regretted that. Space had been the next challenge, the next ultimate step. One that only a few people could reach. And now he had it in the palm of his hand.

What on earth was wrong with him?

He shifted on the step and turned to face her. He didn't have his usual confidence, or his bravado. It felt as if part of his personality were missing. And how well did he actually know Corrine to tell her any of this?

It was almost as if she could hear his thoughts. It didn't matter that she was still mad with him. She set down her plate and turned towards him.

'Is this about the other job?' Her tone was cynical.

She didn't like this. And he could understand. From a professional perspective the candidates were screened to infinity and beyond. Any shadow of doubt should have been revealed during the process and the candidate screened out. To find doubts now would be unusual. And more than anything, it would be costly.

If he pulled out now he'd more or less taken someone else's place. He knew exactly how much he'd wanted to do this. How would he feel if he heard someone had been selected for the team and then pulled out? How would his team members feel if he told them he could no longer pilot for them?

After a few seconds she spoke again. 'The research job—the cancer job. It would be a once-in-a-lifetime opportunity. You could make a difference to millions of people all over the world.'

He was baring his soul here and finding it difficult to meet her gaze. What must she think of him? He sighed. 'Just like being an astronaut is a once-in-a-lifetime opportunity. But would I make a difference for anyone else, or would I just feed my own ego—my own pride that I'd actually made it?'

He let the words hang between them, then let out a wry laugh. 'Of course, there's every chance I could head up this research team, spend billions of dollars and fail miserably. Would that be even worse than being selfish and going into space?'

He finally met her gaze. Her face was still pale. But what was more she'd lost the little spark from her eyes. The one he liked so much.

'There's nothing selfish about going into space. You've no idea the experiments you might be asked to perform there. They might be every bit as important as the cancer work. And what if space is our final frontier? What if we've already damaged the earth too much to reprieve it? Space could be the lifeline for humanity. What you discover in space could help the progression of the human race.'

Wow. He should have guessed. She'd invested her life in WSSA. Of course she could see the bigger picture. Of course she could reach out and imagine the ultimate goal. None of this was about the here and now. None of this was about him and her.

And no matter how confused he was right now he could get that.

It was a stark reminder of how selfish he was being.

But part of him still had doubts. Although he'd aced all his tests in Kazakhstan, part of him still wondered if Austin Mitchell, astronaut, was part of the attraction for Corrine. If he stayed on the job he might be away for six months but, ultimately, he'd come back to Texas and be based here. That might suit her. And he hated the small part of his brain that considered that.

But Corrine definitely seemed unnerved. Her hands had the slightest tremble and she was shifting from foot to foot. She looked as if she had a whole lot more on her mind than just him and her.

He wanted to wrap his arms around her and pull her close. For both of them. But he could almost see the invisible little barriers she'd erected around herself. The wave of emotions he was feeling right now wasn't reflected in Corrine's face. He could feel her pulling away from him.

All of a sudden it hit him. Like a tidal wave.

He waved his hand. 'This isn't about the job, Corrine. It's a flattering offer. But this is much more than a job. This is about choosing.'

This time her look was wary. They'd had this discussion before. She was all about choosing and control.

He sat down on her porch steps and stared out over the fields. He'd thought clearing the air with Corrine would be simple. But he hadn't realised how seeing her again would make him feel.

What he really wanted to do was pick her up and carry her through to the bedroom at the back of the house. But she'd probably drop kick him if he tried that.

'I don't want to turn into my father.' There. He'd said it out loud.

She stepped back from the railing and walked over to the steps, sitting down next to him. 'Okay, you got me. What are you talking about?'

'My father. He's bitter. He's always been bitter. And it's all my fault. It was me that gave him measles and scarlet fever. It was me that lost him his place as an astronaut.'

She stiffened next to him. And he could see it. There was practically a tic along her jawline. 'That's a ridiculous thing to say.'

'Why?'

She stood up and started marching in circles in front of him. 'Because you were a child. You didn't choose to contract those things. Were you vaccinated? Did he *choose* not to vaccinate you? If that's the case then it's his fault— not yours.' She waved her hand as she marched. 'And anyway, WSSA should have been on top of things like that. All their astronauts should have had their blood screened. If they were susceptible, then they should have been vaccinated.' She stopped pacing and looked at him, putting her hands on her hips.

He couldn't work out why she was so mad. Nor could he take his eyes off her bare, slim, tanned legs.

'And if you ask me, that's ridiculous. Your father contracted something he could have got at any point in his life. That wasn't your fault. But you've grown up thinking that it was. How dare he make you feel like that? How dare he put that pressure on you?'

She was getting more riled up by the second. 'He had no right—no right to do that to you at all.'

Austin stood up and put his hands on her shoulders. 'I know that. I do. It's just taken me a little time to get there.'

'So what does that mean? That you, in turn, will put all that on me?'

If he'd been confused before, he was totally lost now. 'No. What do you mean? What are you talking about?'

She pointed at him. 'You. You came into my office and said we had to cool it. You said I'd—' she lifted her fingers in the air '—"distracted" you. You said that your feelings for me had made you lose focus—that you couldn't concentrate on piloting. What kind of a thing is that to say to anyone? So, if you go on your mission in a few years' time, and make a mistake, that could be my fault? I've ruined your mission. I've cost people's lives? Who does that, Austin? Who says things like that?'

Tears were glistening in her eyes and he could feel panic start to swamp him. This was the last thing he wanted. He'd never wanted to hurt Corrine.

And she was right. Everything he'd said had come out wrong.

This was his fault. He'd met a woman who had just blown him away—much more than any space flight ever could. She'd challenged his mind and his heart. He'd felt a connection that he'd never felt before.

And he didn't know how to put that into words.

What a fool.

He could print out his résumé for anyone. His service, his test-pilot status, the tours of duty, the missions he'd flown. Most people were impressed. Most people used the word hero to describe Austin Mitchell.

But here he was, hurting the woman he loved because he couldn't make a decision.

He shook his head. His heart squeezed as a tear slid down her cheek.

He loved her. *He loved her.* He just couldn't tell her.

Because for the first time in his life, Austin Mitchell wasn't brave enough.

Wasn't brave enough to put his heart on his sleeve and ask her if she could love him back.

The risk seemed huge. What if he declared his love for her then decided he didn't want to be an astronaut? How would she react? Would they still have their connection? Would she still want to be with him?

He'd dated lots of women. But maybe his taste was questionable, because most of them had loved having Austin on their arm and telling the world he was a Top Gun instructor. It seemed they'd been more stuck on the title than stuck on him.

But Corrine wasn't one of those women. And what he felt for her seemed so real that he couldn't bear it if she didn't feel the same way.

It wouldn't be fair. If he chose to go into space, then Corrine would be left on the ground. They'd be apart for months.

She shook her head. 'I don't want this to be about me. I don't want any of this to be about me. I shouldn't even enter into this equation. This has to be about you. About what *you* want. About where *you* want to go in your career. You have to leave me on the sidelines. I can't be part of this.'

He understood. He understood exactly what she was saying. 'But you are,' he said simply. 'I spent four weeks in Kazakhstan thinking about nothing else.'

He almost couldn't believe he'd said that out loud. Austin Mitchell didn't do this. He didn't wear his heart on his sleeve. But when he was about to make one of the biggest decisions in his life he couldn't hold back. He had to play with all cards in the deck.

'I can't let you do this.' She stood up quickly. 'You've wanted this for so long. I can't be the reason you're having second thoughts. We don't even know what "we" are, Austin. If you change your mind now you'll end up hating me for the rest of your life. I can't live with that.'

He could hear the emotion flooding through her. She started pacing. 'What if we have a fight in six months and walk away from each other? How would you feel then?'

He stood up next to her and grabbed her shoulders. 'I don't know. I just don't know. That's what's wrong. I'm so used to knowing exactly what I want out of life. All of a sudden, I'm not so sure.'

One minute she was telling him not to include her— the next it was very clear she wasn't happy. It seemed that Corrine was every bit as confused as he was.

He wanted her to push open her front door and invite him in. He wanted to lie in bed next to her, feel the warmth of her skin next to his and discuss what should happen next. Did they even have any kind of future together?

He just didn't know. He wasn't sure she felt the same way he did. And maybe he was reading too much into this. He'd never met a woman who had got under his skin as Corrine did. Maybe this would pass and he just hadn't realised it.

She backed up towards the door. 'You have to make your own decision about what you want. We've had fun. But I don't want to be the reason that you don't go into space. I don't want to be the reason you change your mind about something you've set your heart on. You can't put that on me, Austin. It's not fair.'

What she was saying was reasonable. It was rational. But that didn't explain the way that it hurt. A tiny part of his head wanted her to wrap her arms around him and tell him she didn't care what job he did.

*Where had that come from?*

Together? For ever? A future together? When had his brain started to think like that? Maybe he was crazier than he'd previously thought.

It wasn't that she was putting some distance between them. She was practically building a wall.

'I have to go.' Before he could even blink she rushed up the steps and into the house.

Gone. Just like that.

He shook his head and pushed his helmet back on, swinging his leg over the bike. He'd no intention of going back to base right now. His fellow candidates would be in the bar and expect him to join them.

He wasn't ready for that. Not yet.

Instead, the wide open roads of Texas were beckoning. He could ride flat out for miles around here. Plenty of open spaces. Plenty of thinking time.

And that was exactly what he would do.

She couldn't breathe. Her heart was pounding in her chest, waiting for the sound of the gunning engine to fade into the distance.

After a few seconds she finally heard it. Her legs started to give way and she slid down the wall, the remnants of her dinner spilling onto the floor.

She couldn't tell him. Not like this. Not now.

One minute she'd thought she'd be a single parent be-cause Austin wasn't ready for all this. The next, he was telling her he was considering putting his dreams on hold and might be having second thoughts. *Because of her.*

She felt sick. If she told him about the baby now, it might

force his hand one way or the other. She didn't want that. She didn't want that for herself or for their baby.

If Austin wanted to be with her, then it should be because of her, not because of a baby they'd created together. Relationships like that never worked. And she didn't intend to destroy herself learning that lesson. She didn't want to put her kid through that either.

Rationally, she knew that Austin was a good guy. As soon as she told him about the pregnancy she didn't doubt he would stand by her. But what would that mean?

If his heart was set on space, she didn't want to be what kept his feet planted on the earth.

More than that, if he was having doubts, she didn't want to be a factor at all. She didn't want him to turn around in twenty years' time and tell her she'd ruined his career.

The trouble was, in all this, she hadn't made room for her heart.

She was trying to think of him. To step back and let him make his own decisions—even though he was doing it without all the facts.

But when that broad frame had walked back into her office the other day she'd felt that familiar ache. The one that would be there whether she was pregnant or not.

This was a guy she'd connected with. This was the guy who could make her burst with happiness one second and have her spitting feathers the next.

He was hot. But he was so much more than hot. She felt safe around him. She felt special. She loved the little twinkle in his bright blue eyes that he seemed to save just for her.

The connection felt real. The connection felt so real. And it was the one she'd been waiting for. The one that other people in love told her would happen one day.

And now it had. In a set of circumstances she couldn't have imagined.

Why couldn't her special guy be someone ordinary, someone normal? Not some hotshot pilot who constantly tried to conquer the world. Not some guy with career ambitions that could leave you breathless.

She banged her head back against the wall. But that was all part of Austin. All part of the guy who had stolen her heart. The guy she'd fallen in love with.

A tear slid down her cheek again. Was this what falling in love was like? Was this what she'd waited her whole life to feel? Because right now it wasn't birds singing and unicorns dashing across the sky through multi-coloured rainbows. Right now it felt like a whole host of tangled thoughts and emotions.

Nothing about it was simple.

But everything about it was Austin.

She had to tell him. Of course she had to tell him. But today hadn't been the time or the place. Next week she had her OB/GYN appointment. Maybe things would be a little clearer in her mind by then. Because right now her brain resembled a slurry, muddy watering hole.

One that she had to find a way out of.

# CHAPTER FIFTEEN

THE ALARMS SOUNDED in his helmet and the orange light flashed in front of him.

'Darn it!' He threw down the pistol-grip tool. Except, he couldn't really throw it down. Not when he was in six million gallons of water.

It drifted off in front of him. The voice came through his helmet. 'Well done, Bates. That's the third time you've screwed up that manoeuvre. So, the space station now has no power in that section and you've just added to the space-junk problem.'

Six hours in the neutral buoyancy lab in Houston. The only way to mimic space's unique zero-gravity environment was to build a replica of part of the space station and put it forty feet underwater. This was where they did their extravehicular activities, or spacewalks. All vital training for going to the space station. He'd completed eight successful spacewalks before now. But today?

'Bring him up, guys.'

Failure. He'd have a failure against his name.

Six hours was the maximum time for anyone in the neutral buoyancy lab. It was time to finish.

He hadn't been thinking about Corrine. He hadn't. He wouldn't allow himself to.

But frustration had been building steadily within him

since the day of the astronaut selection four weeks ago. That was the day he should have back-flipped down the corridor.

Instead, the weight that had pressed down on his shoulders had grown steadily. He'd love to pretend it wasn't there. He'd love to pretend it wasn't affecting him. But only a fool would do that.

The crane raised him out of the pool and two of the technical assistants removed his helmet and suit.

'What's going on with you, Bates?'

Austin's head shot up. Adam, the chief instructor, was standing over him. He liked the guy. A real-life astronaut with a world of experience. He'd let him down today.

'What do you mean?'

Adam folded his arms. 'Since the announcement you haven't been yourself. You've put your head down and studied like your life depends on it.'

'Doesn't it?'

Adam brushed off the wry remark. 'You're not yourself. You've lost your bravado. You've lost your cheek. Want to tell me what's going on?'

For a second he felt bad. He respected this guy and wanted to be honest with him. But, in a way, Adam reminded him of his father—the only difference was this guy had actually lived the dream. How could he tell him that he was having doubts? He was more than having doubts? There was no way this guy could relate to that.

He was questioning his decision to be here more and more. Was this really his dream or was it something else? Was he doing this for his father's approval?

He'd never really considered this before. His path had seemed fixed. The navy, a pilot, a Top Gun instructor, and then an astronaut. For the most part he'd been happy.

But his other love, his lab work, had barely been acknowledged by his father.

Work had been everything before. But it didn't seem
like everything now.

But was he really ready to say that out loud?

He gave Adam a half-smile. 'Maybe I'm just taking this
all too seriously. Maybe I'm just turning into the model
astronaut candidate.'

Adam gave a snort as he walked away. 'That'll be the
day.' He paused at the doorway and glanced over his shoulder again. 'My door's always open,' he said before he disappeared down the corridor.

Austin winced. If Adam had noticed a difference in
him, then others would have too. This wasn't fair on anyone.

He needed to make up his mind—and fast.


Four weeks. Four weeks of nothingness.

Of walking in a daze, answering emails, doing routine
tests and trying to remember to eat. She was supposed to
be gaining weight, not losing.

She still hadn't told him. She still couldn't tell him. But
the guilt was eating away at her, along with a whole host
of other things.

Avoidance was easy. She wasn't in charge of his medical care any more. Any sighting was only brief. But that
was all it took to make her heart contract in her chest.

One glance. One whiff of his aftershave. The sound of
his voice carrying down the corridor. All did stupid things
to her. She'd decided she must be allergic. Because any one
of those three things could make her eyes water.

And she hated feeling like that. She hated being vulnerable.

The grainy little image appeared on the screen before

her. 'There we are,' said the sonographer brightly. 'Here are the arms, the thigh bones, the skull, the spine and this little flicker is the beating heart. Everything looks just fine.'

Corrine let out the breath she'd been holding. Now it was real. She could see a tiny heartbeat. Up until that point it hadn't been quite real. She found her voice, anything to distract herself from the fact she desperately needed to go to the toilet. 'How many weeks am I?'

The sonographer nodded her head. 'Give me a few minutes until I take some measurements.' She concentrated on the screen for a few seconds, carefully measuring near the base of the baby's skull, then measuring the femur and total length. After a very long few minutes she said, 'All done. It looks as if you're around eleven weeks.' She smiled at Corrine. 'Does this tie in with your dates?'

Corrine nodded. The first time she'd been with Austin. The date was practically imprinted on her brain.

The sonographer continued. 'I've taken the measurement for the nuchal scan. That, along with your blood test and age, will let us know if your OB/GYN needs to discuss anything with you regarding any other tests.'

Corrine took a deep breath, watching the little picture on the screen. She was having a baby. Now she had a date to put in the calendar. A date she had to be organised for.

And she knew exactly what test the sonographer was talking about. She was talking about the test to see if her baby was at higher risk of Down's syndrome. She hadn't even given any of the really important stuff much thought. It was time to get a hold of herself.

The sonographer pressed a little button to print out a picture. 'It's much too early to tell you the sex. But we need to arrange for further sonograms. We'll do another one around sixteen weeks and a detailed one at twenty weeks. Either one of those could give you the sex if you'd like to find out.' She started wiping the gel from Corrine's stomach. 'I'll let you dash to the toilet now.'

Corrine pressed her lips together and dashed to the bathroom. Instant relief. Thank goodness. But a different sensation swept over her body like a cool breeze. This was real. She put her hand on her stomach. There was no sign. No sign at all. No swelling. No flutterings—it was much too early for those. And although her breasts ached a little she'd had no other signs. No nausea. No vomiting—just a tiny bit of light-headedness if she stood up too quickly or spun around. That was it.

Until she'd actually seen the little heartbeat she'd wondered if it was actually true. Lots of women skipped periods or had light ones—particularly when they used the brand of pill that she did. But now it was time to sit down and take control. The pre-natal vitamins and folic acid she'd started taking would become a regular part of her life. There would be absolutely no alcohol and she would need to avoid a few of her favourite foods.

She leaned her head against the wall of the cubicle.

Confirmation. Absolute confirmation.

Now it was time to tell Austin.

And she was dreading it.

For about ten seconds she'd considered getting a transfer and going somewhere else to have this baby without ever telling him.

But that was ridiculous. It didn't matter how she felt about all this. It didn't matter that the timing sucked. It even didn't matter what his reaction might be.

She'd hate herself if he left the astronaut candidate programme. And he would probably hate her too. Just as long as he didn't hate their kid.

For another ten seconds she'd worried that history could repeat itself. What if their child contracted something infectious and gave it to Austin—ruining his chance of a space mission?

But one quick check of his notes had revealed he was vaccinated against everything possible. Just the way it should be for astronauts. Times had changed.

But what wouldn't change was this baby. It was already here, currently a work in progress.

And it was time to tell him. Whether he liked it or not.

She sucked in some air and blew it back out.

She put her hand on her stomach and smiled. She wanted to be happy. She wanted to be happy she was pregnant and happy that this baby was here.

Did it matter that everything else was a complete and utter mess?

She put her head in her hands.

The hardest part for her came next. What did she want? What did she want for herself and for her child?

Wow. That was so scary. She stood up and came back into the room, nodding to the sonographer and picking up her bag and little picture.

As she walked outside the sun was shining and the temperature was peaking. A bench under a tree beckoned. It had probably been put there especially for the women who'd just been scanned to sit and contemplate life.

And that life had just changed completely. Although the truth was it had changed nine weeks ago.

She'd spent so long only considering herself. She'd spent so long never letting anyone in. How had Austin Mitchell managed to wiggle his way in there?

Stealth. A cheeky grin. Persistence. And a whole lot of *va-voom*.

Too bad he didn't actually want to be there.

She was scared of what came next. Scared of everything actually. She kind of wanted to just wrap herself in a bubble and stay there for the next seven months. Or stay there for ever.

It was pathetic really. A woman with all this training, all this experience, floundering over her own life.

A warm breeze made her hair flutter around her.

She was lonely.

She'd been lonely for a long time.

She'd isolated herself from others. Yes, she had friends. But she'd never really let anyone get as close as Austin.

What she'd had with him felt special. And she hadn't even told him. Probably because she had so much trouble admitting it to herself.

They were too similar. Work had become everything. Four weeks ago he'd walked away from her—walked away from them.

And now she could recognise why. Because he was feeling as much as she was.

He'd even spelled that out. He was braver than her.

But where did that leave her? Did she want single parenthood or did she want to fight for something more?

She wasn't sure that she wanted to be one of those women. One of those women—or men—who had to spend three to six months staring at the stars and wondering if the person holding her heart was safe. They were heroes right alongside their partners. And it was terrifying. Exposing yourself to emotional risk. She had to understand where she was with all that before she went any further. And she had to do it soon.

Because space baby was on its way.

Austin pulled up outside the yellow clapboard house.

For the first time in a long time he was nervous. He'd made a monumental decision. Now, he just had to tell Corrine. Now, he just had to see how she would react.

He'd been away again. Corrine had left him a voicemail saying they needed to talk. Four weeks in deserts, jungles and in ice. And in that time, everything had become crystal clear for him.

He'd messaged her earlier asking her to come for dinner with him. They hadn't seen each other since he'd worn his heart on his sleeve a month ago. It made him feel horribly exposed. A situation he definitely wasn't used to.

She hadn't said anything he wanted to hear. She hadn't told him how she felt about him. But he could hardly blame her. He'd broken up with her. Of course she wouldn't.

He stared at the door for a few seconds wondering how she would be tonight. But he didn't even have time to turn off the engine and walk to her door. Corrine opened her door and stepped outside. She was ready. She'd been waiting. Surely that was a good sign? But she looked a little nervous.

He sighed. She was wearing a simple black dress. Her blonde hair was tousled. She'd never looked more perfect.

But she wasn't smiling. She seemed tense, her shoulders rigid and her jaw a little clenched. He glanced at the single yellow rose sitting on the passenger seat of the car. The gesture he'd thought might be romantic now seemed contrived and ill conceived. He tossed it into the back seat as Corrine walked around the car and climbed into the passenger seat. 'Hi,' she said quietly. It was all he could do not to fixate on her bare, tanned legs filling the footwell.

'Hi,' he replied. 'How are you?'

Her hesitation was fleeting but he still noticed. 'Fine. I've been busy.' She waited until he'd started down the long dirt track. 'Where are we going for dinner?'

'Somewhere a little different. I think you'll like it.' He *hoped* she'd like it. He'd spent about five hours trying to find the perfect place to take Corrine. The perfect staging for what could be the biggest conversation in his life.

'How did the next stage of your training go?' She was twiddling a piece of hair in her fingers.

Small talk.

He paused. It was a natural question. He'd found out Corrine had spent last week focusing on the astronauts currently on the space station. They needed constant monitoring to ensure they all stayed in perfect health. Bone density, blood electrolyte levels, visual acuity all had to be measured while astronauts were in space and all the medical doctors shared the responsibility between them. Corrine had been on duty all this week so she would have been busy.

She placed her hands on her lap and let her thumbs rotate over and over each other. She was just as nervous as he was.

'The training went fine. Jungle, then desert landing, the ocean landing after that, followed by an introduction to Antarctica.'

She shot him a half-smile. 'So, you managed to avoid snakes, dangerous insects and polar bears?'

He nodded. 'Michael managed to come out in some weird rash after a reaction to something. And Taryn tried to catch rainwater using some bizarre leaf concoction and ended up puking. I've no idea what she actually ingested.'

It wasn't nearly as bad as it sounded. All astronaut candidates were left in a variety of settings to hone their survival skills. It was an essential component of their training. There was no guarantee where their re-entry pod would land. The last one had been around two thousand miles closer to Antarctica than anticipated and it had taken more than twenty hours to finally retrieve the astronauts. Survival skills for all elements were essential.

He turned the car onto the highway. The traffic was light. The rush hour had long since passed and the sun was dipping in the sky, sending streams of peach, orange and red across the darkening twilight. It looked as though it was going to be a perfect Texas evening.

If only someone would tell his churning stomach that. He'd already decided the order he wanted to do things.

Speak to Corrine.

Speak to his father.

Speak to Adam.

But how did you tell a woman that lived and breathed WSSA that you were about to leave? And how did you also tell her that part of the reason you didn't want to go to space any more was because you'd fallen in love with her?

In an ideal world he'd have everything. He'd live one parallel life loving Corrine and being the astronaut his father would be so proud of. In the other, he'd fulfil his dreams of leading the cancer research work and still find a way to love and maintain a relationship with Corrine.

That was the thing. In both parallel lives she was the constant. And once he'd acknowledged that piece of the puzzle the rest all seemed to fall into place.

Corrine was staring out of the car, her gaze fixed on the horizon, her fingers still circling over and over. Her nerves hadn't abated. Maybe she knew it was time for them both to put all their cards on the table. Maybe she wondered why he'd invited her out to dinner so formally. The way they'd left things hadn't been ideal.

The shifting sun glared into his gaze for a few seconds. His reactions were automatic, pulling down the sun visor and easing his foot off the gas pedal until he adjusted his gaze.

And then everything in his world shifted.

One second they were rolling along the highway—the next was like the middle of a disaster movie.

Austin let out an expletive and braked sharply, swerving them to the side of the road. She jerked forward, stopped sharply by the seat belt, then thudded back against her seat.

She couldn't believe her eyes. It was almost as if everything were happening in slow motion. The sun's glare seemed to have affected a few drivers. A truck must have clipped one car, causing it to tumble over and over along the highway. The truck skidded, turning sideways and hitting the side of another car, sending it spinning in circles.

Flames shot off the hood of the tumbling car. It hadn't stopped moving yet. But that had no effect on Austin. The car door was flung open and his feet hit the asphalt almost in one movement. Corrine didn't even have time to catch her breath. Austin's running figure was silhouetted against the lowering sun.

She struggled with the seat belt, trying to release it, pulling and tugging as it stayed fast. She took a deep breath and ignored the pull across her stomach, dropping her hands from the belt to release the tension and jabbing the button again. This time it released.

She flung open the car door. 'Bates! Bates! Stop!' He was running straight towards a car that looked as though it could explode any second.

The momentum of the tumbling had slowed. The car landed on its roof once more, then tipped back onto its wheels, rocking back and forth.

It was a crumpled wreck. Corrine glanced at the other vehicles. She had no medical equipment. It was Austin's car—not hers. But she was the one who should be helping here—not Austin. *She* was the doctor. Not him.

But for the first time in her life she was thinking about

more than her life. She was thinking about the life inside her. Doing anything dangerous could put her baby at risk.

She tried to think rational thoughts as she pulled her phone from her bag. She was a doctor. And she had to act like one.

Her brain went into automatic pilot. First, call emergency services. Second, assess the casualties. Third, push aside all crazy thoughts about the father of her baby putting himself in imminent danger and start trying to do the job she was trained to do.

'Bates! Bates!'

She never called him that. She didn't even like his call sign. Which was why, if she was using it, she must think he was crazy.

But it didn't slow his steps for a second. His eyes were constantly scanning the tumbling car, trying to see the occupants. His brain focused. Two passengers. The driver and a kid in the back. Both looked terrified.

The physics and engineering part of his brain tried to ignore the flames. Astronaut candidates knew more about accelerants, fire, combustibles and burn times than just about anyone on the planet. And he was currently ignoring it all.

The car bounced to a stop and his hands were on the crumpled door frame, tugging at the handle. The woman looked unconscious—her head slumped against the airbag. The door wouldn't move. It was jammed solid. He pushed his foot against the frame and pulled again, using his whole body weight.

Still nothing.

There was a whimper from inside. The heat from the burning flames was already conducting through the metal towards him. He banged at the window. Wide eyes in a terrified little face stared at him.

Something fired deep inside him. He couldn't waste a single second.

'Cover your face!' he shouted. He thudded his elbow against the window but it only shuddered. Something flickered in his brain. He ran around to the trunk. With a tug, it opened. Relief. He grabbed the tyre iron and ran back to the window shouting his instructions again.

He smashed the driver's window a second later, putting his hand past the glass shards to try and open the door from the inside. It still wouldn't budge. He could hear Corrine shouting behind him. He turned. She was perched on the driver's footstop of the truck, checking the driver over. She waved her hand at him. 'Move! Now! Get them out!'

He punched the rest of the glass away and heaved his body inside the front of the car, ignoring the searing heat beyond the windscreen, thumping down on the seat-belt release then piercing the airbag to stop it impeding him.

He must only have a few seconds, but if he didn't drag the woman out, he couldn't reach the kid. He put his hand under her arm and hauled. There was no time to consider spinal injuries and neck braces—it wasn't even his field. There was a ripping sound as he pulled her through the window. He stuck his shoulder under hers to try and capture her weight.

'Here!' screamed Corrine. She was only twenty yards away and he ran towards her, leaving the woman at the side of the highway in her capable hands.

He sprinted back towards the car. The little girl was screaming and it was like an ice-cold vice gripping around his heart. It was torturous to hear. He didn't hesitate, just dived straight in through the driver's window again with his hands outstretched towards the back seat. 'Come on, I'll get you out,' he yelled.

There was a flash. A streak of red just as the little girl folded inside his arms.

Then, an almighty crash. The feeling of impact.

And then everything went black.

She'd checked the other two drivers. Both were conscious, breathing and it was probably best to leave them in their vehicles until the emergency services arrived.

As a doctor she was used to emergencies. But most of her emergencies occurred in hospital or medical facilities. The one a few weeks ago at the lakeside had been unusual. She wasn't used to having the role of first responder with no equipment.

Austin was dragging a woman from the burning car. 'Here!' she shouted. She took a few steps forward but was met by him, thrusting the woman towards her as he laid her down on the roadside. He turned to move away and she grabbed at his arm. 'Where are you going?'

'There's a kid still in the car,' he said. Worry lines creased his forehead. His gaze caught hers for the tiniest second. She felt a buzz go through her system, rooting her feet to the spot. No one else on the planet made her feel like this. She'd never felt a connection like this before. And if something happened to Austin she'd never feel it again.

A kid. She'd never talk him out of this and the truth was she didn't want to. He ran straight back to the car while she watched helplessly. What she really needed now was some kind of fire extinguisher. But there was nothing like that around.

He was close. Too close to the flames licking out from under the hood. This was what it must feel like to realise the person you love most in the world was at risk. Whether that be your lover or your child. Right now, a giant hand had just reached inside her chest, grabbed her heart and lungs and was squeezing all the blood and air out of her system.

The woman on the ground coughed and Corrine dropped automatically to her knees. Bile rose in her throat as she checked the woman's airway and pulse. They were fine and Corrine prayed she'd remain unconscious a few seconds longer—she really didn't need to see her kid stuck in this car.

Austin was head first in the car again, calling out to the little girl. Every part of Corrine's body was clenched. She needed him out and she needed him safe.

She needed to tell him about his baby.

There was a flash of red in front of her and a screech of brakes. The impact of metal on metal chilled every bone in her body. Both cars tumbled over and over.

'Austin!' she screamed as if both their lives depended on it.

Because they did.

# CHAPTER SIXTEEN

NOW EVERYTHING WAS WHITE.

And every muscle in his body ached. He blinked. Something wasn't right.

His head was fuzzy and he almost felt as if he were drifting outside himself.

Someone leaned over him. 'Austin? Are you back with us?' His eyes struggled to focus a little.

The speaker, a woman in white, leaned over and pressed his shoulder. 'You gave us a bit of a fright. I don't think the anaesthetist has ever seen anyone have a reaction like that before.'

He blinked again. What on earth was she talking about?

She kept talking, even though he was tired again. 'You're a little swollen because of your reaction to the anaesthetic—that's why you're having trouble seeing right now. We've got you on some steroids. The swelling will settle quickly. All being well, you'll get home tomorrow.'

Tomorrow? What did she mean tomorrow? What day was it? He had somewhere to be, something to do. It was very important. But he just couldn't remember what it was.

The gel on her stomach was cold. There had been no time for the doctor to heat it. There wasn't even a sonographer available. Her heart was pounding and her stomach still twinging. She tried to sit up a little. 'Austin? Have you heard about Austin? And the little girl? How is she?'

The doctor pushed her shoulder back against the trolley as he frowned at the grainy screen and repositioned the probe. 'How many weeks did you say you were?'

Corrine's breath was caught somewhere in her throat. For a few seconds she wasn't thinking about Austin or the little girl. For a few seconds she wasn't thinking about herself or 'them'. Right now she was only thinking about her baby and praying it had survived the accident.

'Fifteen.' The words came out choked.

He pushed the probe lower into her abdomen. 'Ah, here we are.' He lifted a finger and pointed at a flicker on the screen. 'Sorry, I'm only covering tonight. Obstetrics isn't my speciality.'

She let out her breath in a whimper. Her baby—their baby—was still there. She didn't care about work any more. She didn't care about money or how she would cope.

The doctor printed her out a picture. 'Here you go. For reassurance.'

She gulped. The sonographer had given her a picture a few weeks ago. One she'd kept in her purse and looked at over and over again. But this was different. Today had put everything into perspective for her. There were two people in this world she wanted to fight for. She grabbed the paper towel from the doctor and wiped down her own abdomen, swinging her legs from the trolley. Right now she knew exactly where she should be and who she should be with.

She could have lost him. She could have lost the guy she loved—the father of her child—and she'd never even told him that she loved him.

'Which way to Austin Mitchell's room?'

The doctor looked a little stunned. 'You can't leave.

You're still under observation. You should remain on bed rest for the next couple of days.'

She spun around again and gave him her best glare. 'What room is Austin Mitchell in?'

The doctor gulped and shook his head. 'I'm sorry, I don't know.'

Corrine pushed her feet into her shoes and started down the corridor, her head turning from side to side as she checked the names on the whiteboards. Her skin started to prickle. Was there a reason she couldn't find him?

Please, no. Her heart thudded against her chest. Two guys in white coats were standing outside a room at the bottom of the corridor in conversation with a nurse.

As she moved closer she could hear a voice drifting out into the corridor. 'Do you all want to stop muttering out there and tell me what's wrong?'

He sounded annoyed, agitated. And she'd never heard anything so fine in her life.

She didn't even stop to talk to them—just pushed past and walked straight into the room.

'Austin?' His head turned towards her.

Wow. He currently looked like the marshmallow man. Every part of him was swollen. He was almost unrecognisable. But all she felt was instant relief.

It was Austin. He was alive. And he was all in one piece. Sure, she could see some dressings on his arms—he must have suffered some burns. And something else had obviously gone wrong.

She crossed the room in a second and put both hands on his face. He squinted at her. 'Corrine? I was so worried. The little girl? Do you know how she is?'

He blinked as if he was trying to focus. Then he put one hand over hers. Any second now she'd start crying. He must be so uncomfortable right now, but he hadn't even

asked what was wrong, he'd asked about the little girl he'd
tried to rescue.

That was her guy. The guy she loved with her whole
heart.

It was amazing how things could just become crystal
clear. She didn't care if Austin wanted to be an astronaut
or not. She didn't care if he wanted to stay at home all day.
If he completed his training and got the next mission to
space, then she'd teach herself to love long-distance. And
hopefully she'd teach him that too. Whatever he wanted
to do with his life, she wanted to be there. She just hoped
that he wanted her, and their baby, too.

'She's fine, Austin. She's been admitted to Paeds for
observation. Her arm is fractured but there are no other
injuries. She should be fine.'

He frowned. 'Are you okay?'

She hesitated for a second, wondering if she should say
any more. Was now really the time to tell him?

'Mr Mitchell?'

They both glanced around. He dropped his hand from
hers.

The doctor walked over to the bed.

'What happened to him?' Corrine asked.

He held his hand out towards Corrine. 'I'm Dell Cair-
ney. Mr Mitchell's anaesthetist.' He smiled at Austin. 'Mr
Mitchell decided to give us a bit of a fright when we took
him to Theatre to stitch him up and remove all his shrapnel.'

Corrine looked at the IV bag hanging next to her. 'He
reacted to the anaesthetic?'

Dell nodded. 'That would be the understatement of the
year. Let's just say I'm putting a special marker on his
medical notes.' He turned to Austin again. 'The swelling
should be down in a few hours. That's why you can't see

properly right now. All being well you should be able to go home tomorrow.'

'And my vision will return entirely to normal?' He was pressing. Of course he was. This was Austin Mitchell. The man was a superhero, an ace Top Gun pilot and on the top of the list of astronaut candidates.

'I'm a pilot.' His gaze met Corrine's. 'I'm training to be an astronaut.'

He was. And she was going to have to take the bravest step in her life. She was going to have to learn to trust him with her heart.

The anaesthetist nodded to the nurse at the door. 'Take Mr Mitchell downstairs. We need to run another couple of tests to make sure we got every piece of metal out of him.' He winked at Austin. 'Can't have an astronaut going to space with any extra baggage.'

Corrine stepped over to the bed and kissed his cheek. 'Good luck. I'll be waiting for you when you get back.'

Something flashed across his face. A look of regret? Of sadness? She had no idea what was going on inside his head right now.

'We'll talk when I get back?' he said quickly.

She gave him a nod as they wheeled the bed out of the door. This would be the biggest conversation of her life. And she wasn't quite sure where it would end.

Could she really trust her hero with her heart?

# CHAPTER SEVENTEEN

WHEN HE OPENED his eyes again it wasn't Corrine sitting in his room. It was Blair King.

Blair stood up as soon as he realised Austin was awake. 'Lieutenant Commander Mitchell.'

'Dr King.' His words were sharp. He couldn't help it. Where was Corrine?

'You'll be pleased to know everything is fine. The swelling has gone down—you almost look normal again. They've confirmed that they've got all the shrapnel out. You've got around forty stitches, but they should heal without any problems. We'll make arrangements for you to work at the base for the next few weeks. After that you should be able to resume the normal training programme.' He gave Austin a broad smile. 'You're quite the hero, Lieutenant Commander Mitchell. And you're lucky you weren't more seriously injured. You could have ruined your chances of being an astronaut.' He walked around to the other side of the bed. 'I'd say we need to have a chat about your risk-taking behaviour but I know I'd be wasting my breath. By the way, the little girl's mother is doing fine now too.'

Blair was tiptoeing around what he really should be saying.

Austin had no doubt. He'd been more than lucky. He'd

escaped with his life. But in those few milliseconds that the red car had hit them his life had flashed before his eyes.

He'd heard people talk about it before. But he'd never experienced it. Never felt it.

He could have died today and he'd never told Corrine that he loved her. Never told her that he'd made a decision to walk away from all this. If the research job was still available he'd take it. If it wasn't? He'd find something else. Something that meant he'd be near to her.

She was the important factor here and he wasn't afraid to tell her.

'Where's Corrine?' His stomach growled loudly. He hadn't eaten in hours.

Blair pushed a plate of toast towards him. He hesitated. 'She...fainted. I made her go home. She needs some rest.'

Austin was out of the bed in an instant. 'She fainted? What's wrong with her?' This wasn't right. Corrine hadn't been in the accident. She should be fine.

He glanced around the room and tugged at his hospital gown. 'Where are my clothes? Where are my shoes?' He bent down and looked under the bed, ignoring the little shooting pains in his abdomen. No. Nothing there. And nothing on the chairs except Blair King, who was looking distinctly uncomfortable.

He stalked around to the other side of the bed and yanked open the tiny locker. It was stuffed full with a white plastic bag. He grabbed it and emptied the contents on the bed. The waft of burning fuel nearly knocked him sideways. Great. His clothes were crumpled beyond all recognition, were dirty and they stank. He sighed and turned to face Blair. Sure, he could probably punch the guy and steal his clothes but that still wouldn't get him a ride.

'Blair, I need clothes and a ride to wherever Corrine's holed up.'

Blair shook his head. 'What you need to do, Lieutenant Commander Mitchell, is get back into bed and wait for the surgeon to come and speak to you. You haven't been formally discharged yet. This—' he waved his hand towards Austin '—won't help anything.'

Austin stepped towards him. 'Don't make me punch you. Would it help if I told you I quit? I'm not your responsibility any more?'

Blair looked shocked. 'What are you talking about? You can't quit.'

Austin pointed at his eye. 'Really?' His sarcasm was in full flow now. He waved his hand and shook his head. 'Whatever. It doesn't matter anyway. I'd already decided before this. What I need to do now is talk to Corrine. Now, will you help me or not?'

He reached into the pocket of his crumpled trousers and pulled out what he needed.

Blair stepped forward. 'Are you sure about this, Austin? Maybe this isn't the right time to be making any decisions.'

Austin held his hand in front of Blair's face. 'Too late. My decision is made. Now, help me get to Corrine or get out of my way.'

Blair hesitated for the briefest second then let out a sigh and gave his shoulders a shrug. 'Okay, then, let's go.'

Corrine was curled up in a ball on her sofa, drinking tea and watching reality TV. She was nervous—more than nervous. Almost scared to move. Blair finding her lying on the floor had scared the living daylights out of her. She hadn't wanted to leave Austin's side but ever since she'd been handed that little sonograph picture she'd realised how much she had to lose—they both had to lose.

Even though, statistically, she knew lying on the sofa for the next few days wouldn't really lessen her chance of potential miscarriage, she was quite happy to stay here for the next six months if it would give her a healthy baby.

Her door opened. No knock. No noise of a car pulling up. She jumped. Austin's broad frame filled her doorway. He was wearing a blue pair of hospital scrubs.

'What are you doing?' She couldn't actually believe he was here. His footsteps paused. 'What about your wounds?' She took a step towards him.

She could see him swallow as he stepped forward, letting the door bang closed behind him.

'All stitched,' he answered. 'Swelling's gone down.'

'What did they say? Will you have any after-effects?'

He frowned. 'Shouldn't have. I'm sure they told you that.' His voice lowered. 'What's going on, Corrine?'

Her voice trembled. 'What do you mean?'

'They told me you fainted. Are you hurt? Is something wrong?' He moved forward, backing her up towards the sofa, and she sank back down into the cushions. He knelt down next to her, concern written all over his face.

Her stomach twinged again. But this time it was nothing to do with the car accident.

She swallowed. Too bad her tea was finished. Right now she really needed something to drink.

'Not wrong, exactly,' she said carefully.

'What does that mean?'

Her heart squeezed against her chest. She really loved this guy. His charm, his demeanour, his heroics and his values. If she'd been planning to pick a father for her baby, Austin Mitchell would have topped the list every single time.

But she hadn't made those plans and neither had he. Right time or not, she had to tell him.

And it felt like the biggest risk on the planet. She had to tell him everything. She had to be honest. She had to tell him that she loved him and she was prepared to wait. To wait for him to come back from space. She had to trust him with her heart.

She held out the black and white scan picture with her trembling hand. 'This is my news.'

Austin wasn't a doctor but most guys the world over could recognise a scan picture when they saw one.

She held her breath. It only took a few seconds for recognition to set in. His eyes widened, then first a frown, then a broad smile covered his face. He reached forward and touched her abdomen. 'Are you okay? Is the baby okay? The accident. I braked hard. Did I hurt you? Did I hurt him?'

She felt a partial wave of relief. There were no questions. No resentment. Only concern. But could there be more?

She shook her head and pointed to the picture. 'They took the scan after the accident and showed me the heartbeat. Everything's okay for now but they didn't make any promises. I'm supposed to rest the next few days.'

He looked up at her. 'Your news. You said this was your news. Was this what you wanted to tell me the day I got selected?'

She bit her lip and nodded.

'Why on earth didn't you tell me at the time?'

'What? Before or after you dumped me?'

He cringed. But she wasn't finished.

'How could I tell you? You'd just said that thinking about me was putting you off your work—making you lose focus. You implied that thinking about me could make you crash the shuttle you were piloting. I was hardly going to tell you about a baby at that point.'

He was still holding the sonograph picture and his hands had the barest tremble.

'So why tell me now?'

She took a deep breath. 'Because I've had some time to think about it. I was always going to tell you. This isn't exactly something that I could hide and I don't want to hide it.'

She was feeling brave now. She was building momentum. It was easier to get everything out.

'And I guess you're just going to have to learn. To learn how to love someone without crashing a pilot shuttle. And I'm going to have to learn to love someone without killing any patients back here on earth. But this is my first time. And you and I have got a history of first times. So I guess we can do this together.'

She held her breath. Waiting to see what he would say. Praying it would be something good.

He'd closed his eyes for a few seconds as she spoke, but he opened them again and fixed them on her. 'This is the best news I've ever had,' he whispered.

She gulped. Was the best news just about the baby, or was it the fact she loved him?

'Which part?'

He held out his hands. 'All of it.' He stood up. 'It's over.' She was hit by a wave of confusion. His words were firm and clear with only the tiniest hint of sadness. He turned to face her. 'That's why I was taking you to dinner last night. I wanted to tell you I'd made up my mind.'

A thousand thoughts flooded her brain. She wasn't sure if she was suffering from pregnancy brain or being-in-love scrambled brain.

'Made up your mind about *what* exactly?' Her stomach twisted in knots; she hoped her face and voice didn't betray her.

'About the fact I've found a very good reason to keep my feet firmly on terra firma.'

She blinked. Those electric-blue eyes were fixed on her face. Something twisted inside. 'And what reason is that?'

His eyes twinkled. 'It's you, Corrine. It would always be you.'

She felt a little flutter. Darn it. Her heart had just skipped a beat. She so wanted this. She just didn't want to be his default position. So, she had to ask again.

'But you've aced every test. You're first pick for pilot. It's what you dreamed of.'

He shook his head. 'It's what I thought I dreamed of. The reality was a bit different. It's certainly what my father dreamed of and I've listened to him talk about it for so long that I thought it was my dream too.'

Her heart squeezed in her chest.

'I'd already decided. I've found my one. The one that people spend their whole life searching for. And it's you, Corrine.'

She felt her heart swell. She could hear what he was saying but still had questions. 'But lots of astronauts are in love, have families and still go up into space.'

'I know they do. But I choose not to. I don't want to spend six months on a space station away from you. I realised that space just isn't my dream any more. I'm not sure that it ever was. If the research position is still available I'll take it. It might not be in Texas but I can fly back from Maryland every few weeks. That's the longest we'd need to be apart. I love you, Corrine. I don't want to be away from you for even two weeks. And I'm hoping you'll feel the same way and we can make this work. I choose you, Corrine.'

She sucked in a breath. It was everything she wanted to hear but she had to be sure.

'WSSA was your dream from when you were a kid. If you give it up for me...' she laid her hand on her stomach

'...if you give it up for us, at some point you'll resent us. I don't want that. I don't want that for our son or our daughter. I don't want that for us.'

He lifted his hand and stroked her cheek. 'I don't want that for us either. It won't happen. But I can't promise you I won't still be a risk taker. You have to know the only thing I would change about yesterday was that you were in the car with me. I wish I'd never done anything that could have harmed our child.' He gave his head a little shake. 'But no matter what the risks to me I would still have rescued that mom and kid. It's me. It's who I am. I could never, ever walk away from something like that. And I hope that's part of why you love me. Because you know that. You know that I would always be the person to do that and you wouldn't even try to stop me.'

His words struck home. That was exactly how it had been. She'd been scared, she'd been terrified for him, but Austin hadn't hesitated. And maybe she wouldn't love him quite so much if he had. This was the person she'd fallen in love with. And she didn't want to change a single thing about him.

He took a deep breath. 'If the accident hadn't happened last night I would have taken you for dinner, told you that I loved you and that I was quitting. I'd be lying if I said you weren't a part of this.' He pressed his hand against his heart. 'I have to go with what's in here. And that's you.' He let out a laugh. 'And to think I was worried you wouldn't want me if I wasn't an astronaut.'

She frowned. 'What on earth do you mean?' She met his gaze. 'Most people on the planet are praying for a cure for cancer more than they're dreaming of a mission to Mars.' She reached over and squeezed his hand. 'And I'll be proud of you no matter what job you have. *We'll* be proud of you.'

He knelt down in front of her again. 'There was something else I planned to do last night.'

'What?'

He reached into his pocket and pulled out a black velvet box. 'This.'

She held her breath as he flipped open the box. The single diamond was dazzling. And perfect.

A little tear started to slide down her cheek.

'Hey, you're not supposed to cry.'

She laughed and wiped it away. 'I know, I can't help it. Blame the hormones.'

He gave a little nod and pulled the ring out of the box. 'I had something extra embedded in the back of the ring.' His smile reached from ear to ear. 'A tiny bit of meteorite that reminds us of where we met.'

She put her hand on her chest. 'You did?'

He nodded. 'Corrine Carter, I love you with my whole heart. You've made me realise what it is to put someone else first, and I'm going to learn to put two people first. I promise you I'll always let you be in control—except in the kitchen. How do you feel about having a guy without a job as a husband? Because that's what I am. If the research job works out, fine, if it doesn't I promise to do the cooking for both of us. And I'm aiming for the next fifty years.'

He stood up in front of her and she slid her arms up his chest. 'I think, Lieutenant Commander Mitchell, that we can do anything together. And I'm aiming for the next fifty years too. I can't imagine spending a minute with anyone else. I love you, Austin.' She stood up on her tiptoes and whispered in his ear, 'And I promise not to cook for you.'

He picked her up and spun her around. 'Is that a yes?'

'That's definitely a yes!'

He gave a whoop and spun her around again.

He lifted his hand and ran his finger down her cheek.

'So you can live with the fact your husband-to-be isn't going to be an astronaut, he could be an old laboratory guy? You can do this?'

She put her arms around his neck. 'I think laboratory guys are kind of sexy. And of course I can do this. *We* can do this. We can find a way to make this work. You think I'm going to let a guy like you slip through my fingers? Not a chance.' She dropped a kiss on his lips.

'How about a honeymoon in Key Largo? There's a bikini I want to see you in.'

'You'd better be quick. Soon, it'll be the only thing that fits me.'

He ran his fingers through her hair as a broad smile broke out on his face. 'Hey, we'd better start praying that this baby isn't a girl.'

'Why?'

He laughed. 'My great-grandma has been waiting ninety-five years for another girl to be born in the family. It's been boys all the way and she insists that if a girl is born it has to have her name.'

His eyes were twinkling.

She shook her head. 'Oh, no. What's great-grandma's name?'

'Meryl-Felicia.'

She gulped. 'Tell me you're joking?'

He shook his head. 'Nope. And it's been instilled in me since I was a little guy that if I ever had a daughter I'd need to use the family name.'

Corrine nodded slowly and put her hand on her stomach. 'Well, little one, there we have it.' She tilted her head to the side and wound her arms back around his neck. 'Just remember, I haven't met great-grandma yet. Maybe I can charm her.'

He put his hands on her hips and pulled her closer. 'What, the way you charmed me?'

She laughed. 'Maybe I'll bake her a cake.'

He picked her up and swung her around. 'Please. Anything but a cake. I'm sure she'll love you just like I do.'

She smiled as her feet touched the ground again. 'I guess we don't need to go into space to find what our hearts want—it's right here on earth.'

Then he kissed her—just as the hottest man on the planet should.

\* \* \* \* \*

*If you enjoyed this story, check out*
*these other great reads from Scarlet Wilson*

*A TOUCH OF CHRISTMAS MAGIC*
*THE DOCTOR SHE LEFT BEHIND*
*CHRISTMAS WITH THE MAVERICK MILLIONAIRE*
*TEMPTED BY HER BOSS*

*All available now!*

# MILLS & BOON®
## Hardback – May 2016

## ROMANCE

| | |
|---|---|
| **Morelli's Mistress** | Anne Mather |
| **A Tycoon to Be Reckoned With** | Julia James |
| **Billionaire Without a Past** | Carol Marinelli |
| **The Shock Cassano Baby** | Andie Brock |
| **The Most Scandalous Ravensdale** | Melanie Milburne |
| **The Sheikh's Last Mistress** | Rachael Thomas |
| **Claiming the Royal Innocent** | Jennifer Hayward |
| **Kept at the Argentine's Command** | Lucy Ellis |
| **The Billionaire Who Saw Her Beauty** | Rebecca Winters |
| **In the Boss's Castle** | Jessica Gilmore |
| **One Week with the French Tycoon** | Christy McKellen |
| **Rafael's Contract Bride** | Nina Milne |
| **Tempted by Hollywood's Top Doc** | Louisa George |
| **Perfect Rivals...** | Amy Ruttan |
| **English Rose in the Outback** | Lucy Clark |
| **A Family for Chloe** | Lucy Clark |
| **The Doctor's Baby Secret** | Scarlet Wilson |
| **Married for the Boss's Baby** | Susan Carlisle |
| **Twins for the Texan** | Charlene Sands |
| **Secret Baby Scandal** | Joanne Rock |

# MILLS & BOON®
## Large Print – May 2016

## ROMANCE

| | |
|---|---|
| **The Queen's New Year Secret** | Maisey Yates |
| **Wearing the De Angelis Ring** | Cathy Williams |
| **The Cost of the Forbidden** | Carol Marinelli |
| **Mistress of His Revenge** | Chantelle Shaw |
| **Theseus Discovers His Heir** | Michelle Smart |
| **The Marriage He Must Keep** | Dani Collins |
| **Awakening the Ravensdale Heiress** | Melanie Milburne |
| **His Princess of Convenience** | Rebecca Winters |
| **Holiday with the Millionaire** | Scarlet Wilson |
| **The Husband She'd Never Met** | Barbara Hannay |
| **Unlocking Her Boss's Heart** | Christy McKellen |

## HISTORICAL

| | |
|---|---|
| **In Debt to the Earl** | Elizabeth Rolls |
| **Rake Most Likely to Seduce** | Bronwyn Scott |
| **The Captain and His Innocent** | Lucy Ashford |
| **Scoundrel of Dunborough** | Margaret Moore |
| **One Night with the Viking** | Harper St. George |

## MEDICAL

| | |
|---|---|
| **A Touch of Christmas Magic** | Scarlet Wilson |
| **Her Christmas Baby Bump** | Robin Gianna |
| **Winter Wedding in Vegas** | Janice Lynn |
| **One Night Before Christmas** | Susan Carlisle |
| **A December to Remember** | Sue MacKay |
| **A Father This Christmas?** | Louisa Heaton |

# MILLS & BOON®
## Hardback – June 2016

## ROMANCE

# MILLS & BOON®
## Large Print – June 2016

## ROMANCE

| | |
|---|---|
| **Leonetti's Housekeeper Bride** | Lynne Graham |
| **The Surprise De Angelis Baby** | Cathy Williams |
| **Castelli's Virgin Widow** | Caitlin Crews |
| **The Consequence He Must Claim** | Dani Collins |
| **Helios Crowns His Mistress** | Michelle Smart |
| **Illicit Night with the Greek** | Susanna Carr |
| **The Sheikh's Pregnant Prisoner** | Tara Pammi |
| **Saved by the CEO** | Barbara Wallace |
| **Pregnant with a Royal Baby!** | Susan Meier |
| **A Deal to Mend Their Marriage** | Michelle Douglas |
| **Swept into the Rich Man's World** | Katrina Cudmore |

## HISTORICAL

| | |
|---|---|
| **Marriage Made in Rebellion** | Sophia James |
| **A Too Convenient Marriage** | Georgie Lee |
| **Redemption of the Rake** | Elizabeth Beacon |
| **Saving Marina** | Lauri Robinson |
| **The Notorious Countess** | Liz Tyner |

## MEDICAL

| | |
|---|---|
| **Playboy Doc's Mistletoe Kiss** | Tina Beckett |
| **Her Doctor's Christmas Proposal** | Louisa George |
| **From Christmas to Forever?** | Marion Lennox |
| **A Mummy to Make Christmas** | Susanne Hampton |
| **Miracle Under the Mistletoe** | Jennifer Taylor |
| **His Christmas Bride-to-Be** | Abigail Gordon |

# MILLS & BOON®

## Why shop at millsandboon.co.uk?

Each year, thousands of romance readers find their perfect read at millsandboon.co.uk. That's because we're passionate about bringing you the very best romantic fiction. Here are some of the advantages of shopping at www.millsandboon.co.uk:

* **Get new books first**—you'll be able to buy your favourite books one month before they hit the shops

* **Get exclusive discounts**—you'll also be able to buy our specially created monthly collections, with up to 50% off the RRP

* **Find your favourite authors**—latest news, interviews and new releases for all your favourite authors and series on our website, plus ideas for what to try next

* **Join in**—once you've bought your favourite books, don't forget to register with us to rate, review and join in the discussions

Visit **www.millsandboon.co.uk**
for all this and more today!